P9-CEH-715

STORYBOOK COLLECTION

Disney PRESS
New York

Table of Contents

Printed in the United States of America

First Edition

10 9 8 7 6 5 4 3 2 1

G942-9090-6-10046

This book is set in 18-point Goudy Infant.

Library of Congress Catalog Card Number on file

ISBN 978-1-4231-1574-8

Visit www.disneybooks.com

For Text Pages Only

A New Toy

Andy was a young boy with many toys. He loved playing with all of them, but his favorite was Sheriff Woody.

Woody was an old-fashioned cowboy doll with a pull string. He had been Andy's best friend since Andy was in kindergarten. He even had a special spot on Andy's bed where he slept each night.

Woody and Andy had all kinds of exciting adventures together. Andy had a playset of an old Western town. When Woody caught the bandits in town, Andy pulled his string. "Reach for the sky!" Woody would say.

Once the good guys were all safe and the town was peaceful again, Andy would pull Woody's string. "You're my favorite deputy," the cowboy said.

One day, while Andy was playing with his toys, his mother called out, "Your friends are going to be here any minute!"

"Okay," Andy said. "It's party time!"

He ran up the stairs to his room and dropped Woody on his bed. Then he went to the crib and picked up his little sister, Molly.

"See you later, Woody," he called over his shoulder as he left the room.

After Andy and Molly left, the room was quiet for a moment. Then Woody sat up and rubbed his head.

"Pull my string," he said. "The birthday party's today?"

Woody waved at the other toys in the room. "Okay, everybody, coast is clear!" he called out.

Slowly, the rest of Andy's toys came out of their spots in the closet, out from underneath the bed, and out of the toy chest.

Woody dropped down from the bed onto the floor. All around him, toys stretched and chatted, something they could only do when there were no humans around to see them.

Woody looked around the room until he saw the toy he was trying to find. "Hey, uh, Slinky?" Woody said as Slinky Dog approached. "I've got some bad news."

"Bad news?" Slinky Dog cried.

"Shhh," Woody whispered. "Just gather everyone up for a staff meeting. And be happy!"

When everyone was ready, Woody said, "Okay, first item today. . . . Has everyone picked a moving buddy?"

Andy and his family were moving to a new house in one week. Woody didn't want any toys to get lost or be left behind.

Woody made a couple more announcements. Then, when he couldn't hide the bad news any longer, he lowered his voice and said, "Uh, minor note here. Andy's birthday party has been moved to today."

"What?" all of the toys yelled at once.

Woody explained that this was because of the move.

But the toys were worried. Every time Andy got a present, they were afraid it would replace one of them!

"No one's getting replaced," Woody said.

Then Hamm announced that the kids were arriving.

Woody sent the Green Army Men downstairs with a baby monitor. They would radio up descriptions of each present as it was unwrapped.

Andy got a new lunch box and a board game, as well as a few other presents. Then his mother pulled out one last gift.

Before Sarge could give a full report, the baby monitor cut out. The toys were frantic to know what the last present was!

Just then, Andy and his friends raced into the room. Andy dropped the last present on his bed. Then the kids ran back downstairs.

Woody was on the floor surrounded by the other toys. They looked at him, wondering what to do next.

"Let's all be polite and give whatever it is up there a nice, big, Andy's-room welcome," he said.

Woody pulled himself up over the edge of the bed. The last present was a new toy. He was a bright plastic action figure in a spacesuit.

"Howdy," Woody said, "My name is Woody."

"I'm Buzz Lightyear, space ranger," the new toy said.

The other toys crept closer to meet Buzz. They were impressed by his laser and the wings that popped out of his backpack.

LIGHTYEAR

Buzz thought he was a real space ranger, sworn to protect the galaxy from the evil Emperor Zurg. The toys listened to his tales of adventure in awe. Then Buzz showed them how he could fly. He bounced off a rubber ball, rode around a racetrack loop, and swung from a model airplane.

Woody didn't think Buzz was all that special. "That wasn't flying," he said. "That was falling with style."

But no one listened to him. They were too busy helping Buzz repair his spaceship and trying his workout plan.

The other toys weren't the only ones who thought Buzz was a lot of fun. Suddenly, he had become Andy's favorite toy!

Woody looked on sadly as Andy traded his cowboy hat for a space helmet. He replaced his cowboy sheets with new Buzz Lightyear ones. And worst of all, Buzz took Woody's special spot on Andy's bed while Woody slept in the toy chest.

One evening, Andy's mom took him and Molly to Pizza Planet. She said he could bring one toy with him.

Woody wanted to be that toy! He planned to knock Buzz behind the desk where Andy couldn't find him. But instead, Buzz fell out the window!

The other toys glared at Woody. They thought he was trying to get rid of Buzz because he didn't like being replaced as Andy's favorite toy.

"Wait a minute," Woody said. "It was an accident. I can explain everything."

Andy burst into the room before Woody could finish. "Be right down," he called out. "I've got to get Buzz."

When he couldn't find the space ranger anywhere, he grabbed Woody. Then he ran downstairs and hopped into the car.

Buzz watched Andy from underneath a shrub. As the car started up, he ran and leaped onto the car's bumper.

When Andy's mother pulled into a gas station, Buzz jumped into the backseat with Woody.

"Buzz! You're alive!" Woody said excitedly. "This is great! You can tell everyone that this was all just a big mistake." Woody smiled.

Buzz wasn't happy, though. He tackled Woody so hard that they both fell out of the car.

They were so busy fighting that they didn't even notice Andy and his mom get back into the car until it drove off!

"Doesn't he realize that I'm not there?" Woody said as he watched the car disappear. "I'm a lost toy!"

Buzz was talking into his wrist communicator, trying to call for help.

"You're a toy!" Woody yelled at the space ranger. "You aren't the real Buzz Lightyear!"

Buzz shrugged. "You're a sad, strange little man," he said. Then he started to walk off.

DINOCO

Woody wanted to let him go. But just then, a Pizza Planet delivery truck pulled into the gas station.

Woody knew he couldn't return to Andy's room without Buzz. He told the space ranger he'd found a spaceship that would help him get home. The two toys climbed into the truck.

When they arrived at Pizza Planet, Woody led the space ranger over to Andy and his family. They needed to get close enough to hop in the basket of Molly's stroller.

"Okay, Buzz, get ready and . . . Buzz?" Woody turned around to see Buzz striding toward the Rocket Ship Crane Game. He thought it was a real spaceship.

Buzz climbed the game and fell into a pile of toy aliens. Woody followed.

Suddenly, Woody gasped. "Sid!" he said. "Get down!"

Sid was Andy's neighbor. He liked to destroy his toys for fun.

The claw started to move. It clamped on Buzz! Woody grabbed Buzz's foot to hold him down, but it was no use. They were both pulled into the air.

"All right!" Sid cheered as Woody and Buzz dropped into the prize slot. "Double prizes!"

Sid reached into the door to the prize slot and picked up Woody and Buzz. He smiled at his two new toys.

"Let's go home and . . . play!" he said with a wicked laugh.

Woody knew they were doomed. They might be taken apart or blown up! But worst of all they might never see Andy again. . . .

Moving Day

Sid was Andy's next-door neighbor. He wasn't very nice to his toys. He'd take them apart, then attach one toy's head or legs to another's body.

Sid had won Woody the cowboy and Buzz Lightyear the space ranger in a game at Pizza Planet. Woody and Buzz had been at the restaurant looking for Andy.

As Woody looked around Sid's room, some of Sid's toys came out from their hiding places.

"They're gonna eat us, Buzz!" Woody yelled. "Use your karate-chop action."

Woody and Buzz managed to escape from Sid's toys. They ran out into the hallway and came face to face with Sid's dog, Scud. Woody ducked into a closet. Buzz hid in a dark room behind the door.

Suddenly, Buzz heard a voice saying, "Calling Buzz Lightyear. This is Star Command."

Buzz looked up at the TV. The voice was coming from an ad for Buzz Lightyear toys. It continued, "The world's greatest superhero, now the world's greatest toy."

Buzz stared in shock at the TV. He couldn't believe what he had just heard. He wondered if Woody had been right all along. Was he really just a toy?

The space ranger walked out of the room feeling sad. He looked out an open window at the blue sky and watched a bird fly by. He kept hearing Woody's voice in his head saying, "You are a toy! You can't fly!"

He hung his head against the railing over the stairs. Then he had an idea. He would prove to Woody that he could fly. He *was* a space ranger!

Buzz climbed up and stood on the top of the railing. He opened his wings. Then he leaped.

"To infinity and beyond!" he called out.

He hung in the air for a moment and then started to fall. He crashed on the floor at the bottom of the stairs, breaking off his left arm.

When Woody found him, Buzz was upset, but he understood that he was a toy.

Woody was desperate to get them both back to Andy's house. He ran to the open window and called out, "Hey, guys!"

Andy's toys appeared in the window next door. They were surprised Woody was there.

"Oh, boy, am I glad to see you guys," Woody said. "Here, catch this." He tossed a string of Christmas lights over to them so he and Buzz could climb across.

But Buzz wouldn't move. Woody held out Buzz's broken arm to show that he was with him.

The other toys didn't believe Woody. They thought he had hurt their new friend.

Woody felt terrible. When he turned around to tell Buzz, he saw Sid's mutant toys closing in around the space ranger. Woody ran over to hold them back, but they took Buzz's arm and pushed the cowboy away.

Then, after a few minutes, the mutant toys stepped away from Buzz. They'd reattached his arm! Woody couldn't believe it.

Suddenly, the other toys scurried off. Sid was coming! Woody hid under a milk crate, but Buzz wouldn't move.

When Sid walked in the room, he held out a rocket. "I've always wanted to put a spaceman into orbit," he said. Then he taped the rocket to Buzz.

Sid was about to take Buzz outside when he saw a flash of lightning. "Oh, no!" Sid cried. He looked at the rocket. The launch would just have to wait until tomorrow.

All night, Woody tried to convince Buzz to help him escape. He knew Andy's family was moving the next day and they had to get home.

But Buzz didn't care about going home. "Andy's house, Sid's house, what's the difference?" he said. "I'm just a little, insignificant toy."

"Look," Woody said, "over in that house is a kid who thinks you are the greatest. And it's not because you're a space ranger, pal. It's because you're a toy! You're *his* toy."

Woody tried to convince Buzz all night long. But Buzz didn't even move until he looked at the bottom of his boot. Andy had written his name there. Then Buzz knew what he had to do.

He walked over to Woody. "Come on, Sheriff," he said. "There's a kid over in that house who needs us."

Buzz helped Woody out from under the milk crate. Before they could escape, Sid woke up and grabbed Buzz. "Time for liftoff!" he cried as he ran out of the room.

Woody asked Sid's toys to help him. "We're going to have to break a few rules," he said. "But if it works, it'll help everybody." The toys raced outside. Buzz was in position to be launched.

Sid got ready to light the rocket. Suddenly, he heard, "Reach for the sky!" He looked around and saw Woody. He picked up the cowboy.

Then Sid's toys came out from their hiding places in the yard. Soon, Sid was surrounded by all the toys he'd hurt.

Sid looked at the toys around him. As each one came closer, he panicked more and more.

Woody kept speaking to Sid, which made the boy even more scared. "From now on, you must take good care of your toys. Because if you don't we'll find out, Sid." Then Woody leaned in close and pointed at Sid. "So play nice!"

Sid screamed and dropped Woody. He ran into the house and slammed the door. The toys cheered!

Woody helped Buzz down off the launching pad. That's when he saw the moving truck pulling out of Andy's driveway.

Woody ran through the hole in the fence. But the rocket on Buzz's back got stuck. "Just go," Buzz called to Woody. "I'll catch up."

When Woody realized Buzz was stuck, he ran back to help him. The two toys ran down the street chasing the truck. Buzz was the first one there. He grabbed a loose strap and pulled himself up on the truck's bumper. Woody was right behind him.

"Come on," Buzz said. "You can do it, Woody!"

Woody grabbed the strap and started to pull himself up. But something grabbed his boot. It was Scud!

Buzz saved Woody by jumping onto Scud's head. But the truck was moving away quickly.

Woody climbed into the back of the van and rummaged through the boxes. The other toys didn't know what he was doing.

Finally, Woody found what he was looking for—RC Car! He sent RC out after Buzz. But Andy's other toys were upset with Woody. They still thought he'd hurt Buzz, so they pushed him out of the truck.

Then they watched as Buzz and RC picked up Woody. Buzz had the remote control and was speeding toward the truck. The toys realized that it had all been a misunderstanding.

Slinky Dog stretched himself out as far as he could, but they still couldn't get close enough. Suddenly, RC started slowing down. His batteries had run out.

Woody watched sadly as the truck drove away. Then Buzz remembered the rocket on his back. They lit it and zoomed closer to the truck. RC landed easily in the back. But Woody and Buzz were launched into the sky.

Buzz snapped open his wings, and he and Woody broke free of the rocket.

"Buzz, you're flying!" Woody exclaimed.

"This isn't flying," Buzz said. "This is falling with style."

The two toys flew toward Andy's car. They dropped through the open sunroof and landed safely on the backseat.

Andy turned and saw the cowboy and space ranger. "Woody! Buzz!" he shouted. He was happy to have his two favorite toys back.

Woody and Buzz settled into Andy's new house with the rest of his toys. They were happy to be home.

When Christmas rolled around, the toys sat near the baby monitor to listen as Andy opened his gifts.

"You're not worried are you?" Woody asked Buzz.

"No," Buzz replied nervously. "Are you?"

"Now, Buzz, what could Andy possibly get that is worse than you?" Woody teased.

They listened as the first present was opened.

Woof! Woof!

"Wow! A puppy!" Andy cried.

Buzz and Woody looked at each other and laughed. At least it wasn't a toy!

Woody's Big Adventure

"Hey, Woody! Ready to go to cowboy camp?" Andy said.

Woody the cowboy doll was very excited about camp. He'd been looking forward to it for weeks.

Andy grabbed Woody and Buzz Lightyear the space ranger, his two favorite toys. "Never tangle with the unstoppable duo of Woody and Buzz Lightyear!" he exclaimed, linking the toys' arms together.

Just then, there was a loud *RIIIPPP*! Woody's shoulder had a tear in it.

Andy's mom suggested fixing Woody on the way to camp, but Andy shook his head sadly. "No, just leave him."

"I'm sorry, honey," said his mom. "But you know, toys don't last forever." She put Woody up on a high shelf.

Woody looked out the window as Andy left without him. He felt even worse when he discovered Wheezy, a toy penguin who'd been put on the same shelf months ago after his squeaker broke. Woody wondered if that was *his* future, too.

TRIPLE-R

The next morning, the toys spotted something terrifying. Andy's mom had put up a sign for a yard sale!

She looked around Andy's room for items to sell. The toys all watched in horror as she picked up Wheezy.

Woody waited until Andy's mom left the room, then he whistled for Andy's dog, Buster. Together, they snuck outside and rescued Wheezy. But as they headed back to safety, Woody tumbled to the ground. With his injured arm, he couldn't hold onto Buster's collar.

One of the sale shoppers saw Woody and picked him up. Then he smiled with excitement. "Oh, I found him!" he said.

The man grabbed some other items to buy, hiding Woody in between them. But Andy's mother saw the cowboy. She told the man that Woody wasn't for sale.

"I'm sorry," she said. "It's an old family toy." She took Woody and locked him up in the cash box.

As soon as she turned around, the man pried open the box and stole Woody! From their upstairs window, the other toys watched in shock.

Buzz quickly jumped out the window and slid down the drainpipe to rescue his friend. But he was too late. Buzz watched the man's car drive away. The license plate read LZTYBRN.

The man brought Woody home and put him in a glass case. Then he put on a chicken suit.

"You, my little cowboy friend, are going to make me big buck, buck, bucks!" the man said. He flapped his wings and walked out.

Woody knew the man was the owner of Al's Toy Barn. He'd seen him wearing the chicken suit on a commerical for the store.

Woody pushed open the door to the glass case and ran to the door. But he couldn't get out of the apartment.

Suddenly, a toy horse galloped over and a cowgirl hugged him tightly. "*Yee-hah!* It's really you!" she shouted.

She danced Woody around and pulled his string. Then she put her ear to his chest and listened to his voice box say, "There's a snake in my boot!"

"Ha! It is you!" the cowgirl exclaimed. Her name was Jessie. She introduced Woody to the horse, Bullseye, and a toy still in its box—the Prospector.

"We've waited countless years for this day," the Prospector said. "It's good to see you, Woody!"

"Hey, how do you know my name?" Woody asked.

"Why, you don't know who you are, do you?" said the Prospector.

Bullseye turned on the lights to reveal a room filled with things that had Woody's picture on them. Then Jessie showed Woody an old television show called *Woody's Roundup*. Woody was the star!

Meanwhile, back in Andy's room, Buzz and the other toys had figured out who had taken Woody. Buzz came up with a plan to rescue his friend.

"Woody once risked his life to save me," Buzz told the others. "I couldn't call myself his friend if I weren't willing to do the same."

He and some of the toys set off for the store. "We'll be back before Andy gets home," Buzz told the toys staying behind. "To Al's Toy Barn and beyond!"

At Al's apartment, Woody was watching episodes of *Woody's Roundup*. When the show was over, Woody, Jessie, and Bullseye hopped on a spinning record and ran around in circles. *"Whoo-eee!"* Jessie cried. "We're a complete set!"

"Now it's on to the museum!" declared the Prospector.

Woody paused. "What museum?" he asked.

The Prospector told him that as a complete set they were valuable toys. Al planned to sell them to a museum in Japan for a lot of money.

"I can't go to Japan," Woody said. "I gotta get back home to my owner, Andy!"

Jessie gasped. "He still has an owner!" she cried. She shook her head. "I can't do storage again.

"The museum's only interested in the collection if you're in it, Woody," the Prospector said. "Without you, we go back into storage."

ROUNDUP
COWBOY
SUGAR
Woody's
ROUNDUP

Meanwhile, Buzz and his team were almost to Al's Toy Barn. They had one last street to cross, and it was a busy one.

Buzz noticed a pile of orange traffic cones. He instructed everyone to grab one and put it on. Then, slowly, they started to cross the street. Buzz called out directions as they went. "Go!" he said. Then, "Drop! I said drop!"

A car skidded to a halt. *Beep! Beep!* Soon the street was filled with skidding, honking cars, all trying to avoid the moving cones.

Luckily, the toys made it safely.

Inside the store, the toys looked at the many aisles of shiny new toys.

"Whoa," said Slinky. "How are we going to find Woody?"

"Look for Al," Buzz instructed. "We find Al, we find Woody."

Buzz walked down an aisle full of brand-new Buzz Lightyear toys. He gasped when he saw their fancy new utility belts.

"I could use one of those," he said. As Buzz reached out to touch a belt, the new Buzz Lightyear stopped him.

Buzz tried to walk away, but the new Buzz tackled him and put him in a box. Then the new Buzz ran off to join Andy's toys.

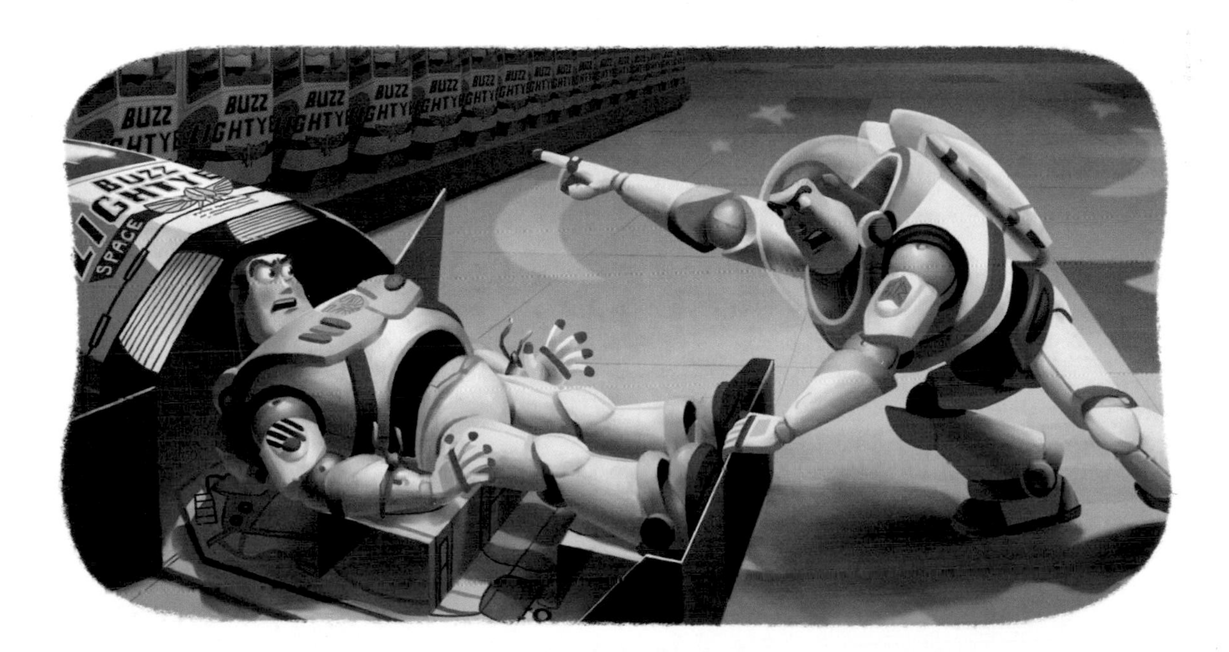

Back at Al's apartment, Jessie was upset that Woody wouldn't go to the museum.

"I'm still Andy's toy," he told her. "If you knew him, you'd understand."

"Let me guess," Jessie said sadly. "Andy's a real special kid and you're his best friend, and when Andy plays with you it's like . . . you feel like you're alive."

Woody stared at Jessie in wonder. "How did you know that?"

"Because Emily was just the same," Jessie replied. "She was my whole world. You never forget kids like Emily or Andy. But they forget you."

Woody felt terrible. "Jessie, I—" he started.

"Just go," she said.

Woody turned and walked away. He didn't know what to do. He didn't want to leave his new friends, but he couldn't help thinking about the old ones.

Meanwhile, the new Buzz and Andy's toys had gone to Al's apartment building. The new Buzz pulled the grate off an air vent for the toys to crawl through. "Come on," he said. "We've got no time to lose."

Since he thought he was a real space ranger, he tried to fly up to the top floor through the elevator shaft! Luckily, the elevator arrived just in time and carried everyone up on its roof instead.

When the toys reached the apartment they were excited to see Woody.

New Buzz grabbed Woody. Slinky wrapped Jessie and Bullseye up in his coils, and Hamm jumped on the Prospector's box.

"Hold it right there!" a voice said suddenly. It was the real Buzz!

The real Buzz tried to get Woody to leave with them, but Woody didn't want to go.

"I can't abandon these guys," Woody explained. "They need me to get into the museum."

Woody told his friends about the old TV show *Woody's Roundup*. He wanted them to understand.

"Woody, you're not a collector's item!" Buzz cried. "You are a toy!"

"This is my only chance," said Woody.

"To do what?" Buzz asked angrily. "To watch kids from behind glass and never be loved again? Some life."

Buzz turned to leave with the new Buzz and Andy's other toys.

Woody looked sadly between the old TV show and Andy's name on the bottom of his boot. He loved Andy. But he didn't want to be forgotten when Andy was all grown up. Wouldn't it be better to be loved by all the visitors at the museum?

A Wild Ride

Woody the cowboy doll watched his friends leave through the air vent. They'd come to bring him home. A man named Al had stolen Woody to sell him and the rest of the Roundup Gang—Jessie the cowgirl, Bullseye the horse, and the Prospector—to a museum in Japan. Woody was ready to go. He was afraid that if he went home Andy would grow up and forget about him. But his friends didn't understand.

Suddenly, Woody realized that he couldn't stop Andy from growing up, but he didn't want to miss seeing it, either.

"Buzz! Wait! I'm coming with you!" Woody shouted.

Woody turned to his new friends and urged them to come with him. But the Prospector blocked the vent.

"No hand-me-down cowboy doll is gonna screw it up for me now!" the Prospector said.

He didn't want Woody to leave. Without Woody, they couldn't be sold to the museum.

Just then, the toys heard footsteps approaching. They quickly moved back to their places.

Al hurried into the room and packed the Roundup Gang in his suitcase. Then he ran out the door. He was late for his flight to Japan. He wanted to sell the toys as quickly as possible.

Andy's toys and the new Buzz Lightyear they had met on the search for Woody all watched in panic from inside the vent.

"Quick! To the elevator!" shouted the real Buzz, hoping to catch Al.

But when they got there, an evil Emperor Zurg toy stood on the elevator roof. Zurg was Buzz Lightyear's enemy. He had seen the real Buzz escape from Al's Toy Barn and followed him to the apartment building.

Zurg attacked with his blaster, and the new Buzz fired back with his laser. Rex was too scared to watch. As the dinosaur turned away, his tail accidentally knocked Zurg off the elevator roof!

With Zurg out of the way, the toys lifted the elevator roof. Al was impatiently waiting to get to the ground floor.

"C'mon," he muttered. "C'mon, c'mon."

Buzz held onto Slinky's legs, and Slinky stretched down to Al's case to undo the latches. Woody popped out of the case and grabbed hold of Slinky's paw.

Just as Slinky Dog started to pull Woody up, the Prospector grabbed Woody's arm tightly and yanked him back inside the case.

Ding!

"Ah, finally!" Al exclaimed as the elevator reached the ground floor. As the doors slid open, the Prospector shoved Woody back down in the case.

Al hurried out of the elevator and ran outside.

Inside the elevator, Andy's toys dropped down from the roof. They watched Al leave. Then the toys ran to the doors, squeezing through them just before they closed.

By the time Andy's toys were outside, Al had already driven off.

They spotted a Pizza Planet delivery truck—and the door was open! The new Buzz went back to Al's Toy Barn. But everyone else hopped into the truck.

Buzz took control of the wheel. "Slink, you take the pedals," he said. "Rex, you navigate."

Rex stood on the dashboard and looked for Al's car. "He's at a red light!" he suddenly shouted. "We can catch him."

Three squeeze-toy aliens hung from the rearview mirror. When the car wouldn't move, they said, "Use the wand of power."

Hamm pushed the gears and the truck sped off.

"Rex, which way?" asked Buzz.

"Right," said Rex. "I mean left. No, right. *Your* right!"

They swerved through traffic and followed Al all the way to the airport.

At the airport, the toys didn't know how they'd get through the crowd without anyone seeing them.

Then Buzz spotted a pet carrier. The toys piled inside, sticking their legs through the small openings in the bottom so they could walk.

"Ahh! Someone's coming!" cried Rex.

It was a little girl. "Oh, a puppy!" she squealed.

Slinky Dog barked a few times to scare her off.

Buzz gave Slinky a thumbs-up. The barking had worked!

At the counter, Al was arguing with the ticket agent.

"I am *not* checking it," he told the agent. He didn't want to lose sight of the suitcase with the Roundup Gang toys.

But he finally gave in. The ticket agent took the suitcase.

Still in the pet carrier, Andy's toys followed the green suitcase into the baggage area.

The toys gasped. There were hundreds of suitcases moving in all different directions. How would they ever find Woody?

"There's the case!" yelled Slinky.

"No, *there's* the case," said Hamm, spotting another green one that looked exactly the same.

The toys split up. When Buzz opened a suitcase, the Prospector jumped up and punched him.

"Hey! No one does that to my friend!" Woody yelled at the Prospector. Woody grabbed him and the two started fighting. Woody's arm was torn in the same spot it had been earlier. Al had stitched him up so he'd be in perfect shape for the museum.

Buzz raced to the rescue.

Woody looked at the Prospector and grinned. "I think it's about time you learned the true meaning of 'playtime,'" he said.

Then Woody and Buzz strapped the Prospector to a pink backpack. He moved out of the baggage area and a little girl picked him up.

"Ooh! A big, ugly man doll," said the girl. "He needs a makeover."

The Prospector was scared. "I've got to get out of here," he said. But it was no use.

Back inside the baggage area, Bullseye had freed himself from the green case, but Jessie was stuck.

"Woody, help!" she cried.

The toys watched as the case was loaded onto a cart.

Woody and Buzz jumped on Bullseye's back.

"Ride like the wind, Bullseye!" Woody shouted.

They raced after the cart. Woody scrambled onto the cart, but it was too late. The green case was already being loaded onto a plane. Woody jumped into another bag so that he could get on that plane. He had to save Jessie!

Once he was on board, Woody jumped out and ran to the green suitcase.

"Excuse me, ma'am," Woody said to Jessie. "But I believe you're on the wrong flight." He grinned.

Jessie's eyes lit up. "Woody!" she cried and hugged him.

"Come on, Jess," said Woody. "It's time to take you home."

Just then, the plane door shut. They were trapped!

The plane started to move. They had to get off!

They found a hatch and crawled down to the plane's wheels. It was hard to stay on, and Woody slipped. Luckily, Jessie grabbed his arm in time.

Woody's hat flew off but it was caught—by Buzz! He and Bullseye were riding alongside the plane. Woody was so happy to see him.

Then the cowboy came up with a daring plan. First he told Buzz to get behind the plane's tires. Then Woody used his pull string as a lasso and looped the end of it around a bolt.

"Jessie!" he shouted. "Let go of the plane!"

"What? Are you crazy?" Jessie shouted back.

But she trusted Woody, so she let go of the plane. Holding on to each other, the pair swung down and under the plane. Woody's pull string unhooked from the bolt. They dropped onto Bullseye's back behind Buzz!

"Nice roping, cowboy," Buzz said to Woody.

Jessie hugged Woody. "That was definitely Woody's finest hour!"

Woody smiled and looked at his friends. "Let's go home."

When Andy returned from Cowboy Camp, he was happy to see his toys. Jessie and Bullseye had joined the rest of the toys to welcome him home.

"Oh, wow! New toys!" Andy said when he saw the cowgirl and the horse. "Thanks, Mom!"

Buzz looked at Woody and smiled. "You still worried?" he asked.

"About Andy? No," he said. "It'll be fun while it lasts."

Toys That Go Bump in the Night

Andy was at a friend's house for a sleepover, so the toys had the whole night to themselves. "What do you feel like doing?" Woody the cowboy asked the other toys.

"How about a spelling bee?" suggested Mr. Spell.

"Nah, you always win," Hamm the piggy bank replied.

"What about a game of hide-and-seek?" asked Slinky Dog.

"I'd rather not," Rex the dinosaur said nervously. He didn't like small, dark places.

Suddenly, rain began pelting the windows. A streak of lightning lit up the sky.

Rex shuddered. "Oh, no!" he cried.

"Reminds me of the newest Buzz Lightyear video game," the space ranger said. "It starts with a storm forcing me to crash-land on a hostile planet. You don't even want to know what happens next."

"Yes, we do," said Bo Peep. "Telling scary stories is the perfect thing to do on a stormy night."

A B C D E F G H
I J K L M N O P Q
R S T U V W X Y Z

"Okay, then," said Woody, "scary stories it is. Gather around, everybody."

"There I am, trapped on a planet filled with six-headed aliens," continued Buzz. "The creatures close in on me. They are ready to blast me with their laser guns. But at the last minute, I activate my jet pack and blast straight up into the sky. Instead of hitting me, the rays from the aliens' guns bounce back off the rocks and stun my attackers while I make a clean getaway."

"Ohhhh!" said the Little Green Aliens.

"Sorry, fellas," said Buzz. "Besides, the aliens in the video game are evil, not nice guys like you three."

"May I go next?" asked Rex.

Rex's story was about the most ferocious dinosaur on Earth. "He had enormous pointy teeth and a fierce roar," Rex said. Then he roared himself. No one jumped or screamed.

"Did I scare you?" Rex asked his friends.

"Sure," Woody replied. He winked at the other toys. All the toys knew Rex was the *least* ferocious dinosaur around. But they didn't want to hurt his feelings.

Rex told the other toys about the creature's bad breath, big eyes, and supersharp claws. "His jaws were like a steel trap!" Rex exclaimed. "He could crush dinosaurs twice his size!" Then Rex shivered with fright.

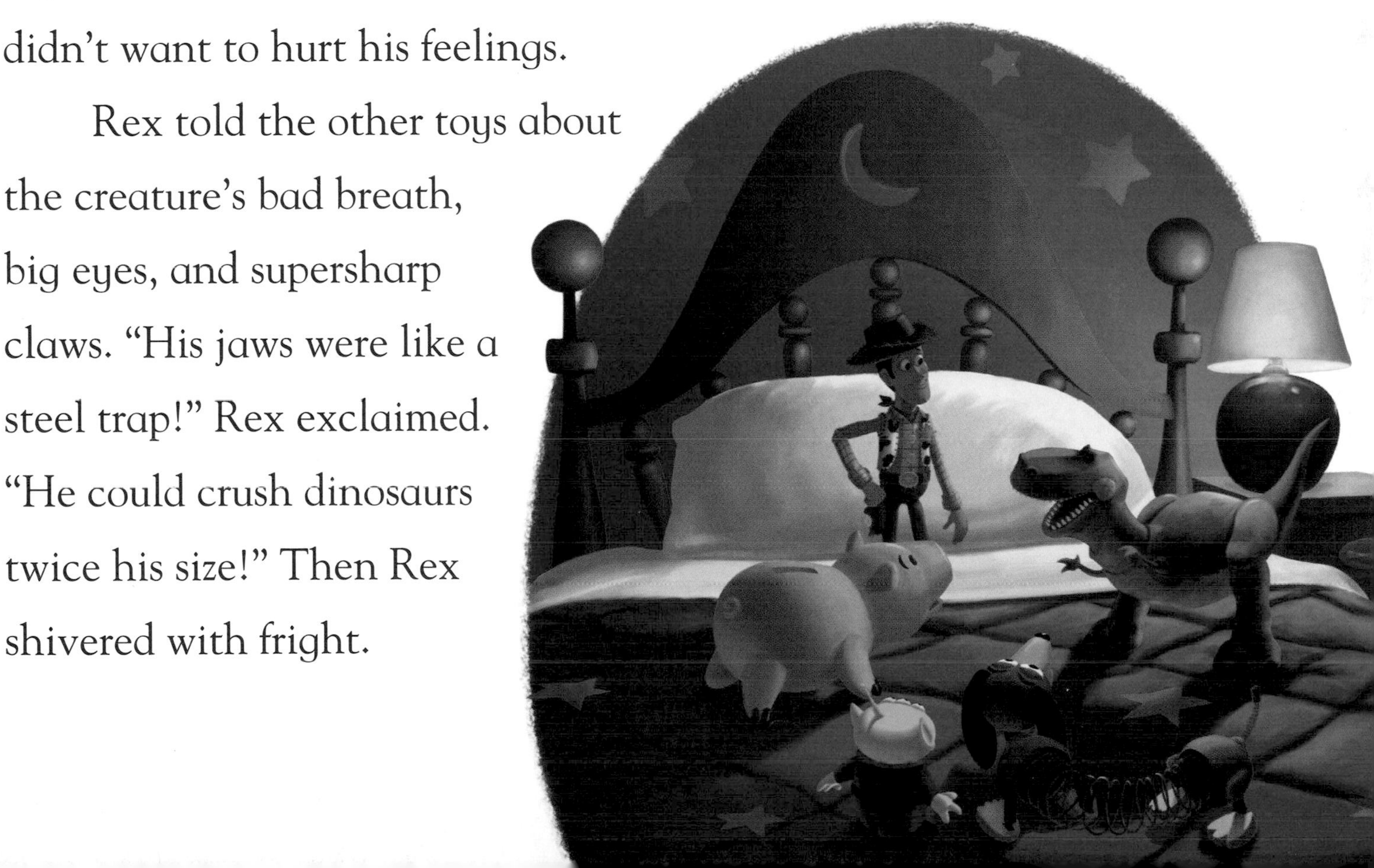

Woody volunteered to tell the next scary story.

"Did I ever tell you guys about the time Andy and I went to a haunted house?" he asked.

The toys all shook their heads. "Well, there we were, walking by a house that was all decorated. Suddenly, these ghosts rose up out of the lawn! Andy ran for the front porch and rang the bell. But a vampire answered the door and he was holding a black cat that had bright yellow eyes."

"W-w-w-what happened next?" Rex asked.

"Then a monster chased us back down to the sidewalk," Woody answered.

He noticed that the other toys looked afraid. Bo had clutched Woody's arm and Hamm was shaking so much that his coins were clinking.

"Don't worry, guys. Andy's brave. And I'm here to tell the tale!" Woody said. "It was all fake!"

"I knew that," said Rex. But Woody could see that his arms were still trembling.

"The people who owned the house set everything up to scare the trick-or-treaters," Woody said. He rubbed his chin. "Maybe that one was a little too scary."

"All right, gang," Woody continued, "I think we've had enough stories for tonight. Let's get some sleep. Andy will be home bright and early tomorrow morning."

Woody had just fallen asleep when he felt a nudge. He moved over a little, but then he felt another small shove.

"Woody! Woody!" Rex whispered.

"Huh?" Woody said groggily. "What is it?"

"I heard something," said Rex. "It's coming from under Andy's bed."

"You must have been dreaming," Woody replied.

"I know I wasn't dreaming, because I haven't gone to sleep yet," Rex explained.

"Maybe it was a noise from the storm," Woody said.

"The storm is over," said Rex.

"You're going to make me get up, aren't you?" asked Woody.

"If it wouldn't be too much trouble," Rex answered.

"All right," said Woody. "Let's go have a look under the bed. You'll see there's nothing to worry about."

When they reached the side of the bed, Woody lifted the bedspread. "It's too dark to see anything under there," he said. "But everything seems okay to me."

GRRRRRR!

"Good job, Rex," Woody added. "If there was anything around here, I'm sure you just scared it off."

"That wasn't me," Rex said, his voice shaky.

"It wasn't?" asked Woody.

Something went *BUMP* underneath the bed.

"Looks like you did hear something, after all," Woody admitted. He was starting to feel a little nervous, too. "Let's go get Buzz before we do any more investigating."

"This had better be an emergency," Buzz declared when Woody woke him.

"I think we have an intruder," Woody whispered.

"What's going on?" asked Hamm.

"It's nothing to worry about," said Woody as calmly as he could. "There appears to be something—or someone—under Andy's bed."

At that moment, a rumbling came from under the bed.

"It sounds hungry!" Rex wailed and then fainted in fright.

The toys crept out of their places in drawers, behind furniture, and in the toy box. They gathered in the center of the room while Woody woke Rex.

Buzz strode confidently up to the bed. "This is Buzz Lightyear, space ranger. You are in violation of Intergalactic Code 36920-Q, which clearly prohibits concealing oneself under another life-form's sleeping unit without prior clearance. It's bad manners. Not to mention creepy. Reveal yourself."

The only response was a high-pitched whine.

"Very well, then," Buzz replied. "You leave me no choice but to take you captive."

Buzz began to crawl under the bed. Suddenly, his space wings shot out and caught on the bedspread.

"I need some help here," Buzz called out. He wriggled around but he couldn't free himself.

"Oh, no!" cried Rex, panicking. "It's got Buzz!"

"Come on, men! We're going in!" cried Sarge. He and the Green Army Men rushed under the bed. They freed Buzz and pulled him back out.

"There's something under there," Buzz replied. "And it was definitely moving."

"We'll take over from here," Sarge announced. "Men, we're going to execute a sneak attack and surround the enemy. You know what to do. Now go, go, go!"

The soldiers split into groups and stormed under the bed.

"Halt!" boomed Sarge's voice. "It's one of our own! Switch to rescue-mission protocol!"

The other toys all looked at each other. "What's going on?" called Woody. "Who is it?"

But there was no answer. All the toys heard was the soldiers moving around under the bed.

"Push, men! Push!" commanded Sarge. "Now, one . . . two . . . three . . . heave-ho!"

Suddenly, RC Car shot out into the room.

"What was he doing under there?" asked Woody.

"His batteries are nearly out of juice," Sarge reported. "He just sat there revving his engine, spinning his wheels, and going nowhere."

"I knew there had to be a reasonable explanation," said Rex.

Woody smiled and patted his friend on the back. "You're right, buddy," he said.

Meanwhile, Buzz had removed RC's battery door.

"The supply truck's coming," Sarge told Buzz. "Let's go, men!" he commanded his soldiers.

Soon, RC was zipping around the room, good as new.

"Don't we feel silly?" said Hamm. "All of us so afraid, and it was only RC."

Just then, Mr. Spell lit up. "A low battery is scary!" he said. "In fact, I am feeling . . . a . . . bit . . . sluggish . . . myself."

"Make a note, Slinky," said Woody. "Tomorrow, fresh double-A's all around!"

Tuned In

Andy's toys were gathered around the TV in Andy's room. They had gotten used to watching TV with Andy when he was home sick for a few days. The set was still pulled up next to the bed, which made it easy for the toys to turn on.

"*This* again," Bo Peep said one afternoon as a superhero show came on. "We watch this every day."

"So?" said Hamm the piggy bank. "He's the defender of the universe! What could be better? I *love* this show."

"Yeah!" agreed Rex the dinosaur. "He is one *super* hero!"

Woody the cowboy doll wasn't impressed, though. "Honestly, I don't know what Andy sees in these shows," he whispered to Buzz Lightyear the space ranger.

"Me, neither," agreed Buzz. "Call him a superhero? A few space rangers with a laser cannon could vaporize that masked man in a nanosecond, no problem."

Woody sighed and shook his head. "They just don't make TV shows like they used to," he said.

"Shows like what?" asked Buzz.

Woody grinned. "Shows like *Woody's Roundup*, of course!"

"Oh, *no*." The toys groaned. When Woody got started talking about *Woody's Roundup*, it was hard to get him to stop!

Woody's Roundup was an old show. It had been on TV when Andy's mom was a little girl. Woody had been the star—along with Jessie the cowgirl and good old Bullseye the horse. The show was always fresh in Woody's mind. Sometimes an episode aired on the Western Channel, and Woody made sure to catch it.

"Now that was a show, wasn't it?" said Woody to Jessie.

"You bet it was!" said Jessie. "Yippee hi-yi-yo!"

"Remember how it started?" Woody went on.

"You bet I do!" said Jessie. She took out her lasso and began to twirl it. "Get over here, Bullseye!" she called.

Bullseye quickly galloped over. Then the three of them smiled and waved to the other toys, pretending they were a captive audience.

"Howdy, pardners!" Woody hollered. "Welcome to *Woody's Roundup*!" He jumped on Bullseye's back. "*Yeehaaah!* Giddyup!" he cried.

While Jessie twirled her lasso and Woody and Bullseye galloped around, Rex picked up the remote control lying on Andy's pillow.

"I've always wondered how this works," he said as he pressed a button.

Suddenly, the channel changed to a *real* dinosaur show.

"Aghh!" cried Rex, diving under the covers. "Save me!" he called.

Immediately, the Green Army Men sprang into action.

"Eliminate the enemy!" Sarge ordered. "Go! Go! Go!"

One after the other, the soldiers jumped on the remote, and right away the channels began to change.

"Ooooooh!" cried one of the Little Green Aliens as the channels flew by in a blur.

"Space and time at last are one!" exclaimed another Little Green Alien.

"Perhaps this machine can help us return to our planet," they said all together.

They moved closer to the screen. "We come in peace," they told the television. "Aliens do not anger TV."

Bo Peep chuckled as she watched the aliens. "They think they can get into the TV," she whispered to Woody. "They're so cute."

Buzz walked over to Woody. “Sheriff, I think we need to put an end to this channel surfing,” he said. He pointed to the Green Army Men, who were balancing on the buttons of the remote.

Woody agreed. He was growing impatient with the flashing channels.

The flipping channels were beginning to drive the other toys crazy, too.

"Sarge, call off the troops!" Woody cried out. "I'm going to be sick from all the flashing."

"Stand down, soldiers!" Sarge commanded.

Buzz marched over to the remote control. "I'll take that," he said. Then he turned to the aliens. "I'm sorry to break this to you, guys," he told them, "but the TV cannot return you to your planet."

The Little Green Aliens looked up to Buzz, thinking he would know how to help them get home. "Oooh," the aliens said at the same time.

"However, the TV can take you to plenty of new places," Buzz continued. He held the remote control and carefully studied the buttons. "I know I saw a show about space somewhere back there," he declared. "All I have to do is figure out how to find it again."

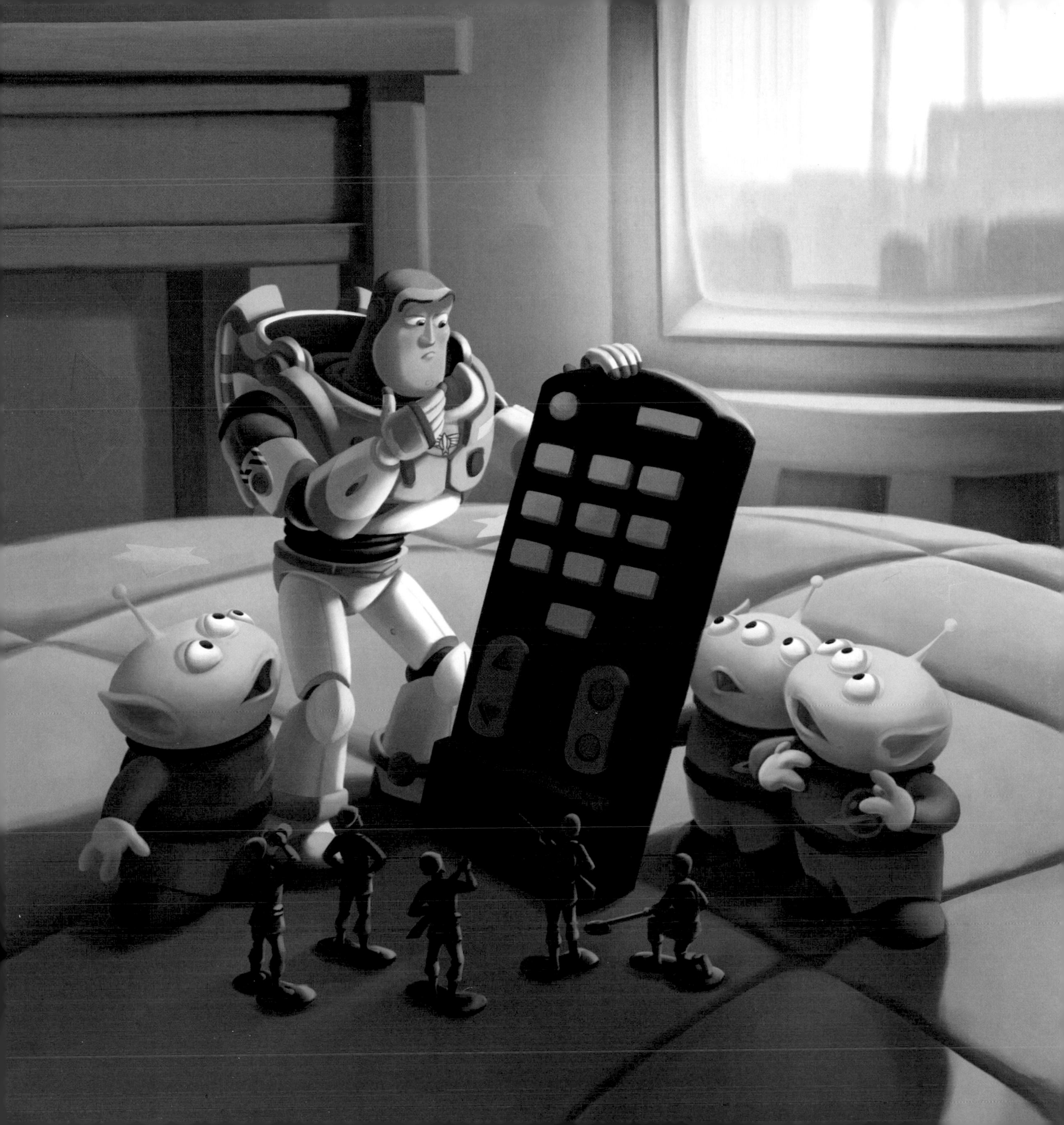

"Now," said Buzz, "which button changes the channel?"

Bo Peep looked over his shoulder. "I think it's—" she began.

Buzz held up his hand. "No, no. Don't tell me," he said. "I'm good with buttons. I bet it's this one." He punched a button. But instead of changing the channel, the sound blasted from the TV. The toys all covered their ears.

"Agghhh!" they yelled.

Since he couldn't reach his ears to block out the noise, Rex dove under the covers again. "Save me!" he cried.

"What did I do?" asked Buzz. He dropped the remote on the bed.

Bo Peep carefully reached around him with her staff and gently turned down the volume.

Buzz sighed with relief. "Thanks, Bo," he said.

"Enough playing around, already," Hamm said. "Let's turn back to the superheroes before Andy gets back."

"But we can watch that show anytime," Slinky Dog complained. "I think we should watch the Animal Channel instead."

This started all the toys thinking about their favorite shows. They couldn't decide what to watch!

"I'd like to watch the Fairy Tale Channel," said Bo Peep.

"How about the Military Channel?" said Sarge.

"Or the Cooking Channel!" said Rex.

"Or the Cowboy Channel!" said Jessie. "We can watch a real-live rodeo!"

"Well, I guess there's just one way to decide what to watch," Hamm declared.

"How?" asked Rex.

"Ask the TV?" said the Little Green Aliens.

"No," Hamm said. "We'll take a vote."

But voting didn't work out as they had planned.

"Uh-oh. The vote is split. What do we do now?" asked Rex.

"Recount!" said Buzz.

"Just a minute," Bo Peep said. "We could vote a hundred times, and the count would be the same. We each want to watch something different. So why don't we watch a little of each channel?"

The other toys smiled. "That's a good idea!" they said.

They watched superheroes for Hamm, who knew the lines so well he could say them along with the characters. They watched the Animal Channel for Slinky Dog. Then they turned to the Military Channel for Sarge and the Green Army Men. They watched the Cooking Channel for Rex. Then, finally, they turned to the Cowboy Channel for Jessie.

"Howdy, pardner!" they suddenly heard Woody say.

"Could ya keep it down, Woody," said Hamm. "We're trying to watch TV."

"Huh?" said Woody. "I didn't say anything."

"Well, would you look at that!" said Jessie, "Woody and I are on TV!" The Cowboy Channel was showing an episode of *Woody's Roundup*!

"Now *there's* a show!" said Woody.

And everyone else had to agree!

A Fine Feathered Friend

Woody the cowboy was watching TV one morning while Andy was at school. His favorite show, *Woody's Roundup*, was on. He liked to watch himself, his horse Bullseye, Jessie the cowgirl, and the old Prospector rustle up some adventure in the Old West. . . .

In the town of Dry Gulch, Sheriff Woody was repainting the old jailhouse. He was always looking for ways to spruce up the town.

A large drop of paint dripped off his brush. "Look out Bullseye!" Woody called to his horse.

Splat! Bullseye looked up just as the paint landed on his forehead. He whinnied.

"Sorry, fella," Woody said as he climbed down from the ladder. He pulled out his handkerchief and wiped off the paint.

Bullseye whinnied again and stomped the ground.

"Not today, pardner," Woody said. "I've got to finish painting and then I'm helping Miss Tilley with her errands."

Bullseye snorted. Most mornings, he and Woody worked together. They rode out to Rattlesnake Ridge to round up cattle rustlers. Or they would patrol the town watching for bandits. But lately, it seemed like Woody was too busy to work with a partner.

Bullseye decided to go find Jessie. She always had time for fun. He heard Jessie's *yo-de-lay-ee-hoo* as he trotted over. She was feeding peanuts to a squirrel.

"Howdy, Bullseye," she said.

Bullseye walked over to Jessie. He bent his front legs so she could climb on his back.

"Oh, sorry, Bullseye," she said. "I promised to help this little guy gather some nuts for his friends. Some other time, fella."

Bullseye started walking back to town. He caught up to the Prospector, who was pushing a brand-new wheelbarrow. Bullseye whinnied.

"Hee-hee. Hello there, Bullseye," the Prospector said, chuckling.

Bullseye stopped and stomped his hoof on the ground. The Prospector usually asked Bullseye to bring his gold-mining pans down to the river. Bullseye hoped he would give him a load to carry.

But the Prospector kept walking along. "I'm gonna find me enough gold to fill this here wheelbarrow," he said.

Bullseye sadly lowered his head to munch some grass. He felt very lonely. Suddenly, he saw something sitting among the weeds. It was a brown speckled egg. Bullseye looked around for a mother hen, but there wasn't anyone in sight.

He found an old basket by the side of the road and nudged the egg inside it. Holding the handle between his teeth, he walked very slowly back to town.

"What a cute little hen's egg," Jessie said when Bullseye passed by her.

Bullseye swished his tail happily and trotted into the barn. Jessie followed him. Bullseye put down the basket and grabbed a mouthful of hay for the nest.

"It's hard work to help an egg hatch," Jessie said. "You'll have to keep it warm and watch out for snakes and raccoons. Then when the chick hatches, you'll have to care for it like its real mom. Do you think you can do it?"

Just then, Woody and the Prospector walked into the barn.

"Bullseye found an egg!" Jessie said. "He's building a nest and is going to help it hatch."

Woody smiled and patted Bullseye on the back. "That sounds like a great idea," he said.

But the Prospector wasn't so sure. "Whoever heard of a horse hatching an egg?" he said. "It's plain ol' foolishness if you ask me."

Woody pulled Jessie and the Prospector aside. "I think Bullseye's been a little lonely lately," he whispered. "This will cheer him up."

Jessie nodded. "It'll be a good thing to keep him busy," she agreed.

Bullseye cared for the egg just like a mother hen. He tucked hay around it to keep it warm. He stayed up all night to chase away raccoons and snakes. He wouldn't leave the egg for a minute.

Finally, one afternoon, Bullseye heard a tapping sound. *Tap-tap-tap.*

It was the egg!

He watched it closely. *Tap-tap-tap.*

A little beak poked through the eggshell. Then—*Crick! Crack!*—the egg broke open!

A tiny yellow chick with spots on its back stood where the speckled egg once sat.

Bullseye whinnied so loudly that Woody jumped out of his sheriff's chair. The Prospector was so startled he fell into the stream while panning for gold. Jessie missed the cow she was trying to rope and lassoed the mailman instead. They all rushed to the barn.

"He's a handsome little fella," Jessie said when she saw the chick in the nest.

"Oh, horsefeathers!" the Prospector said. "Whoever heard of a horse hatching an egg?"

Woody laughed. "Wait a minute. Horsefeathers! That's a great name!"

"Neigh," Bullseye whinnied.

The chick looked up at the horse. Then he opened his beak and said, "Neigh!"

Everywhere Bullseye went, Horsefeathers followed. He perched proudly on top of Bullseye's head as they walked around town. All the folks in Dry Gulch liked to see the horse and chick together. "Howdy, Bullseye," they'd call out cheerfully. "Howdy, Horsefeathers."

"Neigh!" Bullseye and the chick would answer together.

Horsefeathers tried copying everything Bullseye did. He tried sleeping standing up, but he fell in a heap in his nest. He ate hay just like the horse, even though it didn't taste very good to him. He learned how to trot and gallop just like a horse!

One afternoon, Bullseye and Horsefeathers met Woody and Jessie at the corral. Horsefeathers trotted around the ring after Bullseye. Soon the two friends started playing tag. Bullseye trotted after the little chick and touched his tail with his nose. Then Horsefeathers said, "Neigh!" and chased Bullseye until he could pull his tail with his beak.

The Prospector arrived just in time to see Horsefeathers bucking like a bronco. *"Yee-haaaah!"* he cried. "Let's enter Horsefeathers in the Dry Gulch rodeo!"

Jessie looked worried, though. "Horsefeathers should be learning how to be a chicken, not a horse," she said quietly to Woody.

Woody rubbed his chin. "Maybe it's time to find out if Horsefeathers has a mom nearby."

Jessie watched the two friends whinny and chase each other.

Then she nodded slowly. "Maybe we *should* look for a mom," she said sadly. "But I haven't got the heart to do it."

Early the next morning, Horsefeathers hopped onto Bullseye's head. "Neigh!" he chirped.

Bullseye opened his eyes. It was still dark outside. But the little chick was waking up earlier and hungrier each day. Bullseye grunted. Then he got up and led Horsefeathers outside to find some breakfast.

While Bullseye chased a little green worm, Horsefeathers wandered off, pecking the dirt. A dark shadow flew over him, then circled back. When Horsefeathers looked up, he saw a hawk swooping down toward him. Horsefeathers tried to gallop away, but the hawk was gaining on him.

Suddenly, the little chick heard the sound of thundering hooves.

"Neigh!" Bullseye whinnied as he raced between the hawk and the chick. He reared and whinnied as the hawk flew off screeching.

Jessie and Woody ran over, having heard all the noise. Jessie scooped the little chick up in her arms. "That was close," she said to Bullseye. "You shouldn't leave Horsefeathers alone out here."

"You've done a fine job, pardner," Woody told his horse. "But raising a chicken is a little odd. Horsefeathers needs to be with his real family."

Bullseye snorted. He bent down for the little chick to hop on top of his head. Then he and Horsefeathers walked away from Woody and Jessie.

"I didn't mean to hurt his feelings," Woody said to Jessie. They followed Bullseye down the road.

Just then, Bullseye paused to let a mother hen and her chicks pass by. Woody and Jessie came to a stop beside him. They watched the chicks follow their mother, chirping all the way.

Woody looked at Horsefeathers, who was perched on top of Bullseye's head. The little chick didn't seem to notice the others at all. Then Woody heard the strangest sound.

"Peep! Peep! Peep!"

It was Horsefeathers! For the first time, the little chick had chirped like a chicken.

Bullseye leaned down and Horsefeathers hopped to the ground. The little chick looked at the hen. Bullseye nudged Horsefeathers with his nose.

Then the hen spotted Horsefeathers. *"Bok!"* she squawked.

Horsefeathers ran over to his mother and she tucked him under her wing.

"Neigh!" Bullseye called out his good-bye.

"Neigh!" Horsefeathers chirped back. Then he walked off with his mother and brothers and sisters.

One morning, the whole gang went to visit Horsefeathers at the chicken coop. Bullseye was excited about seeing his friend.

When they reached the pen, Woody called out, "Howdy, folks!"

A few speckled chickens looked over.

"I can't tell which one is Horsefeathers," the Prospector said.

Bullseye whinnied. Suddenly, a handsome rooster dashed out of the chicken house and galloped around the other birds.

"That's Horsefeathers!" Jessie pointed out.

"He is one unique bird," Woody said, shaking his head.

"And Bullseye is one unique horse," Jessie added. She gave Bullseye a hug. "Good job, pardner!"

Rocket Launchers

Woody the cowboy doll stood at the window in Andy's bedroom, peeking outside at the school bus. He heard the front door slam downstairs. Then he saw Andy run down the driveway, his backpack bouncing behind him.

Andy stepped onto the school bus, and the bus quickly pulled away.

Woody watched until the bus turned the corner and was out of sight. Then he turned around and looked at the other toys in Andy's room. "All clear!" he announced. "Andy's off to school."

The toys gathered on the floor in the middle of the room, surrounding a long cardboard box. Andy had brought it home the night before. Woody climbed down from the desk and walked over to the box. "Now," Woody said, "let's get a look at whatever this is."

Woody flipped open the box flaps and looked inside. He saw several rubber tubes and a tall plastic stand.

"What's in there?" Slinky Dog asked. He nudged Woody and looked inside.

"I'm not sure, Slink," Woody said. He pulled a piece of paper out of the box. After a couple of minutes he smiled. "It's a rocket launcher," he said.

"How far do you think it goes?" Rex the dinosaur asked.

"There's only one way to find out," Buzz Lightyear the space ranger replied. He started to lift pieces out of the box.

Woody helped Buzz put the rocket together. When it was finished, Buzz said, "Now, who wants to go first?"

"I do!" Jessie said as she jumped up and raised her hand.

Buzz showed her what to do. There was a pump attached to the launch pad. Jessie stepped on the pump as hard as she could, and the rocket shot up into the air. It floated for a minute before landing lightly on Andy's desk.

"Cool," said Hamm the piggy bank. "Can I try?"

"Sure, everyone can try," Woody said. He climbed up onto the desk and pushed the rocket off.

When it was all set up again, Hamm stomped on the pump. *Whoosh!* The rocket shot all the way across the room.

"Look at that," said Rex. "The harder you stomp, the farther it goes."

Soon all the toys wanted to see how far each of them could make the rocket fly.

Buzz and Woody helped set up the rocket for each toy and then measured the distance the rocket flew with the string from a yo-yo. Some toys launched the rocket straight up in the air, while others aimed for the desktop or the door to Andy's room.

"Looks like we have a tie," said Buzz after all the toys had taken a turn.

"Yep," Woody agreed. "Hamm and Slink both made it all the way to Andy's door."

"We need a tiebreaker!" Jessie said.

"That's a great idea," Woody replied. He helped Buzz set up the rocket, then they turned to face the other toys.

"What about best out of three?" Rex offered.

"That'll take too long," Jessie said. She was eager to see who the winner would be.

"We could do one final stomp," Buzz suggested. "That puts the pressure on Slink and Hamm."

"That's okay," said Slinky Dog.

"Yeah," agreed Hamm. "One more stomp sounds good to me."

Woody held his hands behind his back. Slinky Dog and Hamm had to guess how many fingers he was holding up to see who would go first. Slinky picked five and Hamm guessed three.

"Five is right! Slinky goes first," Woody said, holding up his wide-open hand.

Slinky Dog walked over to the rocket. He stretched his body and rolled his head from side to side to loosen up. When he was ready, he nodded to Buzz.

"Okay," Buzz announced to all the toys. "This is it, the big stomp. Slinky and Hamm will each try to launch the rocket as far as they can by stomping on the pump. They only get one try. Whoever's rocket flies the farthest is the winner."

The other toys fell silent as they watched Slinky Dog step up to the pump. Slinky lifted his front paw. *"Grr,"* he said as he pushed down on the pump as hard as he could. The rocket didn't move.

Slinky Dog looked at the rocket sitting on its stand. "What happened?" he asked.

"I don't know, Slink," Buzz said as he walked around the rocket. "It looks like it's all set up correctly. I don't know why it didn't move."

"Maybe Slinky should try again," Rex suggested.

"Or Hamm could go," Jessie said.

Hamm walked up to the rocket as Slinky Dog backed away. "I'll give it a try," he said.

He counted to three and then stomped his foot on the pump. But the rocket still didn't move.

"Well, now we know something's wrong if no one can make it move," Woody said as he walked up to the rocket. He looked at Buzz. "What do you think happened?"

Buzz smiled. "I think we have some space invaders," he said. He walked around the side of the rocket and opened a small door.

The three Little Green Aliens peered out at Buzz and the rest of the toys.

"Hey, guys," Woody said. "What are you doing in there?"

"Go to Earth," the aliens said together. One of them pointed toward the corner of the room by Andy's desk.

Woody looked at Buzz, confused. Buzz looked over at the desk and saw a globe sitting on top. Andy had been using it the night before for a school project.

Buzz helped the aliens climb out of the rocket. "Sorry, guys," he said. "You're already on Earth. That is just a tiny scale model of the real—"

"Um, Buzz," Woody interrupted. He knew Buzz could ramble on about the galaxy for hours. "Can we get back to the contest? Slinky and Hamm want to see who can shoot this rocket to the moon!"

The other toys clapped and cheered, ready to get the contest back underway. Slinky Dog stretched again as he waited for Buzz to give him the all-clear. Then he stepped up to the pump.

Slinky Dog stomped on the pump as hard as he could. The rocket shot off the stand and flew across the room.

"Oooh," the Little Green Aliens said as they watched it fly.

"Good job, Slink!" Woody said.

"That'll be a tough one to beat," said Rex, who had scurried across the room after the rocket. He waited by it while Woody measured the distance with the string.

Hamm stepped up for his turn. Rex was waiting across the room, where Slinky Dog's rocket had landed, to show Hamm how far his had to go. Hamm stomped on the pump and his rocket shot into the air. Everyone held their breath as they watched it fly. Then it landed . . . in the same place Slinky Dog's had!

"Another tie!" Jessie yelled. "What do we do now?"

Slinky Dog looked at Hamm. Hamm looked at Slinky. "What if we give the aliens a ride?" Hamm suggested.

"That's a great idea!" Woody exclaimed as the aliens cheered.

"Ride into space," they said as they shuffled back over to the launching pad.

"You'll have to go one at a time," Buzz said as he helped the first alien into the rocket. He stuck a handkerchief into the small space around the alien. "Can't hurt to have some extra cushioning," he said.

For the rest of the morning, the aliens rode one at a time in the rocket. Each of the toys took a turn stomping on the pump to see how far they could make the aliens fly.

When the other toys got tired of playing with the rocket, Buzz and the aliens sat beside the globe.

"Well, fellas," Buzz said, "what did you think about your rocket ride?"

"Fun," they said. "Tomorrow we go home."

"You *are* home, guys," he said.

"How are our space invaders doing?" Woody asked as he walked over. "Slinky and Hamm were just saying that they think if they worked together they could launch all three of you in one go."

"Oooooh," the aliens said.

Buzz stood up and gave Andy's globe a spin. "There's a plan," he said. "Teamwork will get us out of the galaxy, to the moon—"

"To infinity and beyond!" Woody finished.

Catching Gold

One cold winter day, Woody the cowboy sat in front of the TV with his horse, Bullseye. They were watching his favorite show, *Woody's Roundup.*

"This sure makes me wish it were hot and sunny out there," Woody said as the episode began.

The Roundup gang was going fishing. Prospector Pete was hoping to find gold while Woody and Jessie the cowgirl fished for their lunch. Woody led the gang down to the river.

"Yeeeeehah!" Jessie yelled when she saw the rushing waterfall. "I bet there'll be tons of fish jumping today!"

She wasn't the only one who was excited. The Prospector grabbed his gold-mining pan and went down to the water's edge. "I've got a hunch there's some gold in this riverbed!" he exclaimed. "And I aim to find it!"

Woody smiled as he sat on the bank and cast his fishing line. He was hoping for a good catch.

Jessie went for a walk to look for some wildflowers. Woody stayed in his favorite fishing spot. He hadn't had a single bite yet, but he was still hopeful.

The Prospector walked along the river's edge in search of gold. Soon he came to a shallow pool. He held out his gold-mining pan as he leaned over the water. He began to sift through the sand from the riverbed.

When the water had all sloshed out, he looked at the empty pan. "Hmm," he said. "No gold here."

He decided to try a new spot. He climbed up the rocks next to a nearby waterfall. Carefully balancing on one of the rocks, he scooped up some water and sand in his pan. But there was still no gold.

"I don't understand," the Prospector said, scratching his head. "I just *know* there's gold in this here river."

The Prospector headed back up the river to where Woody was fishing.

"Any fish yet?" the Prospector asked him.

"Nope," replied Woody. "I forgot how long it can take to get a bite. What about you? Any gold?"

Just as the Prospector was about to answer, he saw something shiny in the water. He stepped closer to take another look.

"Eureka!" he cried. "I see gold!"

He jumped into the river with his gold-mining pan. *Splash!* He tried catching the gold with his pan, but it kept sliding back into the water.

"Come help me, Sheriff," the Prospector shouted. "This is the slip-slidin'est gold I ever saw! It doesn't want to be caught!"

"Sure thing!" said Woody. He set down his pole and leaped into the water with the Prospector. Together they dove after the gold. But each time, they came up empty-handed.

"Wait! I have an idea," said Woody. He held up his hat. "We can use these!"

"Good thinking," said the Prospector.

They both used their hats to try to scoop up the swirling bits of gold. The hats made their work a little easier, and they were each able to catch a few pieces of gold.

Just then, Jessie came over to the river's edge. She'd heard all the commotion. She leaned over a rock and was surprised to see her friends diving into the water with their hats.

"What's going on?" she asked. "What are you two doing?"

"Catching gold!" said Woody.

Jessie took a closer look inside their hats, and then she began to laugh.

"What's so funny?" asked the Prospector. "We're going to be downright rich from this batch alone!"

Jessie smiled. "Take a look at your catch," she said.

Woody and the Prospector looked at their hats. They were surprised to see goldfish swimming around!

"I can't believe it!" Woody laughed. "The Prospector was looking for gold, and I was looking for fish."

Jessie looked at the fish leaping out of their hats and giggled. "I guess you both found what you were looking for!"

Little Lost Sheep

Rex the dinosaur had spent the whole morning thinking up jokes to tell the other toys. He wanted to make his friends laugh until Andy got home. They're going to be in stitches! he said to himself.

He looked around Andy's room. Woody the cowboy doll, Buzz Lightyear the space ranger, and Slinky Dog were near the bed, laughing. He walked over to them.

"Hi, fellas," Rex said. Woody and Buzz were still laughing at whatever Slinky Dog had just finished telling them. "I see you are fans of comedy. Would you like to hear one of my jokes?"

"Sure, Rex," Woody said. "We love to laugh."

"Okay, here goes," Rex said. "What do you call a dinosaur that's hungry for breakfast?" He looked from Woody to Buzz to Slinky Dog. Then he said, "An egg-asaurus!"

"Rex, did you come up with that yourself?" Woody asked with a smile.

Rex nodded.

Buzz slapped Rex on the back. "Well done, Rex. Very funny."

"Really?" Rex had thought that was his best joke, but he had plenty more to tell, too.

Before he could begin another one, though, Bo Peep came running over. "Oh, Woody! Something terrible has happened!" she cried.

"What is it?" Woody asked.

"It's my sheep!" Bo cried. "I can't find them anywhere!"

"Are you sure?" asked Woody. "Where did you see them last?"

"They were with me when Andy and I were playing on his bed earlier," Bo said. "But they're not there now."

"Hey, everyone!" Woody called out. "Bo's sheep are missing! Anyone seen them?"

"No sheep up here!" Jessie called down from the nightstand.

Sarge and the Green Army Men quickly pulled together a search party. One by one, the Army Men hopped up onto Andy's bookshelves and checked behind each book. "Negative, Sheriff!" Sarge called down when the search was complete.

Hamm the piggy bank poked his head over the side of a plastic crate where he'd been searching. "I don't see any sheep either."

"Oh, no," Bo said. "Woody, what if I can't find them?"

Woody put his hand on Bo's shoulder. "We won't rest until those sheep are safe with you! Right, everyone?"

The toys began to shout—they all wanted to help.

E
H
T

"All right, everyone, we'll need to search all of Andy's room," Woody said. "Hamm, you check the toy box."

"Sheriff, I think we may need to expand our search to other parts of the house," Buzz said.

"Great idea," Woody replied. "Sarge, can you and your men search Molly's room?"

"Ten-four." The Green Army Men ran out the door.

"Wheezy, you and RC patrol the halls," Woody said. The penguin hopped onto the remote-control car and they zoomed out the door.

"We would like to look in the bathroom," said the three Little Green Aliens.

"Great!" said Woody. "And Buzz and I will search the kitchen. Now let's find those sheep!" Woody and Buzz ran out the door.

"Please, find them!" called Bo Peep. Then she sat down. She looked like she was about to cry.

Rex walked over to her. "Don't worry, Bo," he said. "I'm sure Woody and Buzz will find your sheep soon."

"Thank you, Rex," she said, but she still looked sad.

If only I could cheer her up somehow, Rex thought. "Say," he said. "I don't suppose you would like to hear a joke, would you?"

"Well . . ." Bo said.

"Oh, good!" Rex said. "What do you call the place where sheep get their hair cut? A *baa-baa* shop! Get it?" Rex waited for Bo to laugh.

Bo looked up at Rex. "But sheep don't have hair. They have wool. Oh, I hope they're all right!"

That didn't seem to cheer her up at all, thought Rex.

Rex and Bo heard a rustling sound coming from the toy box. Soon they saw Hamm's face appear over the edge.

Bo stood up. "Did you find anything?" she asked.

"Sorry, Bo," Hamm said. "I looked in every nook and cranny of this thing. There are many toys in there, but no sheep."

"Oh," said Bo. "Well, thank you for trying."

The baby monitor crackled on the dresser. “This is Sarge reporting from the baby’s room. There are not—I repeat, there are not—any sheep in here. Over and out.”

“Oh, dear,” said Bo. “Where could they be?”

“Maybe they’re out looking for the perfect joke, like me,” said Rex. “How about this one to take your mind off your troubles?”

Bo Peep didn’t respond, but Rex continued anyway. “Okay, here goes. Two sheep walk into a dollhouse. One sheep says, ‘Wait, where’s Fleecy?’ The other sheep says, ‘I don’t know. I thought he was with *ewe*.’”

Bo Peep sighed. “Lost, just like my poor little sheep.”

"I'm sorry, Bo," Rex said. "I guess I'm not doing such a good job cheering you up."

"I'm just so worried," Bo said. "But it is still nice to have a friend with me."

Just then, Woody and Buzz came into Andy's room with RC and Wheezy behind them.

"Kitchen is clear," Buzz said. "No sheep were found."

"And nothing in the hallway, either," said Wheezy.

"Maybe the aliens are having better luck in the bathroom," Woody suggested. "Wheezy, can you and RC go over there and find out?"

"Sure!" Wheezy said. Then they zipped out the door and down the hall.

In the bathroom, the aliens were searching through the cabinets.

"Up there!" the first alien said, pointing. High on a shelf near the sink was a fluff of white.

"Sheep!" the aliens all said together. They hurried over to the shelf and began climbing, giving each other a boost to get to the next shelf. Finally, they reached the shelf.

The first alien tried to pick the sheep up, but fluffy white balls flew everywhere. There were no sheep. Just cotton balls!

"Strange," the second alien said.

The first alien picked up a cotton ball. "Ohhh," the aliens all said together. Then they came up with a plan.

A few minutes later, Wheezy and RC rolled into the bathroom. "Did you find anything?" Wheezy called to the aliens. But he didn't see them.

Baa. Baa. Wheezy heard the sound of sheep bleating. He turned. "Sheep!" he cried. "We've been looking for you everywhere."

Wheezy led the creatures toward the door. "It's time for you to go back to Bo Peep," he said.

RC sped in front of Wheezy.

"Go spread the word, RC!" he said. "We found them. We're heroes!" He followed the sheep out into the hall. "Now what could have happened to those aliens?" he wondered.

"We found your sheep!" Wheezy announced when he got back to Andy's room.

Bo Peep gasped and ran over. "These aren't my sheep," she said.

"What?" Wheezy said.

Woody put his hand on the first sheep's wool. He lifted a cotton ball off a little green head. "It's the aliens," he said.

"Guys, *acting* like Bo's sheep won't replace the sheep that are still missing," Woody said.

"Wanted to help," they said at the same time.

"Thank you," Bo Peep told the aliens. "But I'm afraid Woody is right."

Suddenly, Hamm called out, "Andy's mother is coming!"

"Positions, everyone!" Woody said. All the toys found the places where Andy had last left them and went limp.

Andy's mom walked into the room, humming to herself. She placed a basket on the bed and started folding Andy's clothes. After putting away most of his laundry, she looked in the basket and stopped humming.

"What's this?" she said. She took something out of the basket and laughed. She'd found Bo Peep's sheep!

"Hey there, little guys!" she said. "I hope you enjoyed your bath. Now where do these belong?" She looked around the room, spotting Bo Peep on a shelf.

"I bet you missed these," she said to Bo, laughing. "*Little Bo Peep has lost her sheep*," she sang.

Andy's mom placed the sheep right next to Bo. Then she picked up her basket and left the room.

When the toys knew it was safe to move, they burst out laughing.

"You were in the laundry the whole time?" Bo said to them.

"Why is everyone laughing?" Rex said. "Andy's mom didn't even tell a joke!"

"Oh, Rex," Bo said. "Now that my sheep are back, I'm definitely in the mood to laugh. Why don't you tell me one more joke?"

Rex perked up. "My pleasure. Knock, knock."

"Who's there?" the other toys replied.

"The interrupting sheep," Rex said.

"The interrupting—"

Baa! Bo Peep's sheep bleated before anyone could finish. And this time, they all laughed.

The Longest Day

"Could I have everyone's attention, please?" called Woody the cowboy doll. The toys in Andy's room quickly gathered around him.

"What is it?" Rex the dinosaur asked anxiously.

"Don't tell me there's another yard sale!" Wheezy the penguin exclaimed.

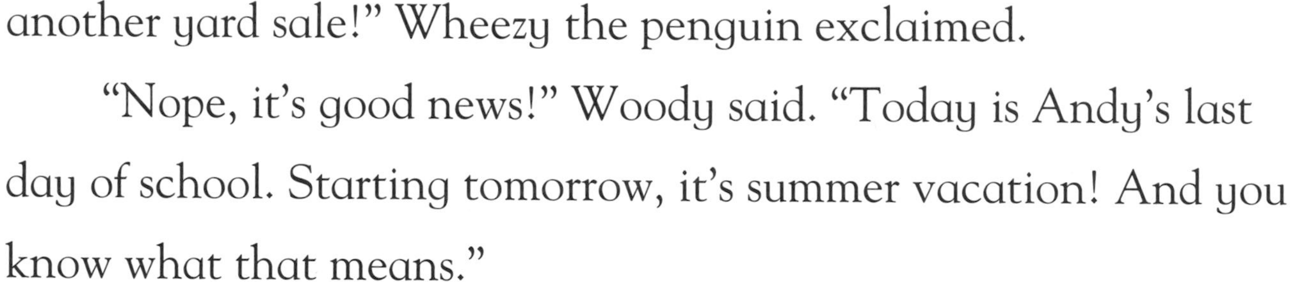

"Nope, it's good news!" Woody said. "Today is Andy's last day of school. Starting tomorrow, it's summer vacation! And you know what that means."

"We get to play with Andy and Molly all day, every day!" Jessie the cowgirl said. *"Yee-hah!"*

"I love summer," added Hamm the piggy bank. "Remember all the fun we had last year?"

"Sure do!" said Slinky Dog. "How about when Andy bounced Woody on the new trampoline!"

Woody laughed as he remembered bouncing over and over. "That sure was something," he said.

"My favorite part of last summer was when Andy set up a dinosaur jungle in the sandbox," said Rex.

"There's no doubt about it," said Woody. "Summers with Andy are the *best*."

"I want vacation to start *right now*," said Hamm impatiently.

"I know how you feel," said Woody, "but we've got a whole morning and afternoon to get through first. We'd better keep busy."

"How about playing Roundup?" cried Jessie. Bullseye the horse whinnied excitedly. He loved that game!

"Okay," said Woody. "Everybody grab something you can use as a lasso. Then try to round up as many objects as you can."

The toys scrambled to find something to use as a lasso. Rex found some dental floss, and Bo Peep found a broken rubber band. When everyone was ready, Woody called out, "Get set! Go!"

Rex had trouble with the floss. "My arms are too short to get any distance," he cried. "All I can lasso is myself!"

Bo Peep lassoed her sheep, and then Hamm.

Wheezy managed to lasso the Little Green Aliens and RC Car with his string. Jessie, meanwhile, was racing around on Bullseye, roping everything in sight!

CRASH! The lamp on Andy's nightstand came tumbling down. "Uh-oh," said Jessie, "I got a little carried away."

"We have to get this cleaned up before Andy gets home," Woody declared. "Could I have all the trucks over here, please?"

Woody attached some ropes to the trucks. "Take it away, fellas!" he called. The trucks slowly lifted the lamp back onto the nightstand. Then Woody climbed the fire truck's ladder and put the lamp shade back in place on top of the lightbulb.

"Sorry," Jessie said.

"Don't worry," said Woody. "Besides, now we're closer to Andy coming home."

"But it's still only morning," Rex protested. "This is the longest day of my life!"

"Don't despair, Rex," Buzz Lightyear the space ranger said. "There are plenty of other things we can do to take our minds off waiting."

"Like what?" asked Rex.

All eyes were on Buzz. "Hmmm," he said. He crossed his arms, accidentally pushing one of his buttons. A red light shot across the room. That gave Buzz a great idea. "What about a round of laser tag?" he asked.

"Okay," said Buzz. "Here are the rules: I chase after you, and if my laser hits you, you're out. Everybody got it?"

"You can't catch me," Slinky Dog taunted. He ran until the front half of his body was stretched clear across the room, but his back half was still standing right in front of Buzz.

"Tag!" shouted Buzz, beaming his light on Slinky Dog's tail. "You're out!"

"Aw, nuts," said Slinky Dog. "I'm just not built for this game."

"What's the matter, Buzz?" called Woody. He was riding on RC. "Are we too fast for you?" They zipped this way and that while Buzz tried to tag them.

"Woody, look out!" shouted Buzz.

"Trying to distract me, eh?" Woody replied. "Well, I'm not falling for that old trick." As soon as the words were out of his mouth, he and RC slammed into the wastebasket and wiped out.

"Tag," said Buzz as he shined his beam on each of them.

After they'd cleaned up the mess from the wastebasket, the toys decided to play hide-and-seek.

They took a vote to see who would be "it." They picked Hamm.

"One, two, three . . ." he counted as everyone hid. Woody and Wheezy scurried into the closet. Rex and Buzz ducked under the bed. Bo Peep and her sheep tucked themselves beneath a cardboard box. Soon, not a toy was left in sight.

The toys waited . . . and waited . . . and waited, but Hamm didn't come to look for them. Woody realized Hamm had stopped counting a long time ago. He stuck his head out of the closet and heard a low, snoring sound. Hamm was asleep!

"Hamm!" shouted Woody. "Wake up!"

"Oh, sorry," said Hamm, "I didn't get much sleep last night. I tossed and turned, and every time I moved, my change made an awful racket."

"The important thing is, you're awake now," said Woody. "Now go find those toys."

"Ready or not, here I come!" Hamm called. He walked off to look for the toys.

He found Rex first. The dinosaur's tail had been easy to spot sticking out from under the bedspread.

Finally, the only toys still hiding were Sarge and his men.

"Maybe they went on a mission," suggested Woody.

Hamm climbed up on the desk and stuck his head out the window. "Sarge!" he yelled, "are you there?"

"Negative!" cried Sarge, appearing on the drawbridge of a castle made of building blocks. The rest of the Green Army Men began popping up on balconies and in tower windows.

"Wow! Neat castle!" said Rex.

"Andy built it last night," Woody explained.

"Say, could we play knights-and-dragon?" Rex asked hopefully.

"Hmmm," said Woody. "But who would play the dragon?"

"Me! I could do it!" volunteered Rex.

"And who would play the knights?" Woody said.

"Request permission for me and my men to play the knights defending the castle from the fire-breathing dragon," shouted Sarge.

"Permission granted," Woody replied. "Let the battle begin!"

Rex pretended to attack the castle again and again, letting out a roar each time. Sarge and his men were always able to push him back over and over.

Then suddenly, Andy's puppy, Buster, came skidding into the room. When he saw the toys inside the castle, he attacked it for real!

"Bad Buster!" Woody said as the dog ran out of the room. He hurried over to the mess and helped the Green Army Men out from under the blocks.

"What are we going to do now?" said Rex looking at the mess.

"We're going to have to rebuild the castle so it looks exactly like it did before," Woody replied.

The toys worked together restacking the blocks. When they were finally done, the castle looked as good as when Andy built it!

Woody looked over at the clock. "We've still got a little time before Andy gets home," he said. "What else can we do?"

"I need to spruce myself up," Bo said as she peered in the mirror. She fixed her bonnet, which had been sliding off her head.

"I'm tired!" Rex said. "Building a castle is hard work."

Woody agreed. The toys all took some time to rest so they'd be ready to play again when Andy got home.

By three o'clock, the toys were all waiting anxiously for Andy.

"What's taking him so long?" Hamm wondered aloud.

"I'm positive this is the last day of school," said Woody. "But let me check the calendar." Woody climbed up on the desk.

The rest of the toys waited on the floor, eager to hear what Woody would say. When Woody came back to the edge of the desk and looked down, the other toys knew the news wasn't good. "I'm sorry, guys," he said. "There's a note on the desk. It appears there's a party after school."

"So what time will Andy get here?" asked Rex.

"I don't know," said Woody. "Look, it's only a few more hours, and then we'll have the whole summer with Andy."

While the other toys drifted off to find something to do, Woody stretched out to sleep. The happy shouts of children filled his dreams. Suddenly, someone was shaking him awake.

"Woody!" cried Bo. "Wake up!"

JUNE

Woody opened his eyes. He could still hear children's voices. He looked out the window and saw lots of kids in Andy's backyard. He wasn't dreaming, after all! Andy's entire class was here for the end-of-school party! No wonder it took him longer to get home, Woody thought.

Footsteps thundered up the stairs, and Andy and his classmates burst into the room.

"Wow! Great toys!" a boy shouted as he picked up Buzz and Rex. The other kids grabbed more toys until Woody and all his friends were part of the celebration.

This is going to be the best summer ever! Woody thought happily.

Woody's Quest for a Date

Woody the cowboy doll sat down and sighed. The rest of Andy's toys were across the room, listening to Bo Peep read a story. Woody wanted to join them. But he didn't feel like he should.

"What's got you so down?" Buzz Lightyear, the space ranger, asked as he sat down next to Woody.

"It's Bo Peep," said Woody.

"What about her?" Buzz asked, confused.

"I don't know," Woody said. He shrugged. "I've been thinking lately that I need to do something to impress her."

"Hmm . . . something to impress a lady?" Buzz rubbed his chin. "When was the last time you saw Bo excited by anything?"

Woody looked at Buzz and smiled. "When you showed us all how you could fly," he said. "Buzz, do you think you could teach me?"

"Of course!" Buzz said. "To Bo's heart and beyond!"

Before they started to practice, Buzz warned Woody that flying could be dangerous. "You must always be alert," Buzz told his friend. "The wind can shift and push you off course. Or if your wings get caught—"

"Buzz," Woody interrupted. "Can we get on with the actual flying?" He didn't want to waste another second.

"Yeah, let's get this show in the air," Rex the dinosaur said. He'd come over to watch along with Hamm the piggy bank and Slinky Dog.

"Okay then," Buzz said. "Strap on your wings."

He helped Woody put on the wings they'd made out of paper. The paper was glued to some rubber bands.

Woody looked back at the wings. He started to wonder if they were sturdy enough to help him fly. But before he could say anything, he was pushed forward.

"Time to take flight!" Buzz called.

Woody landed on the floor with a thud. "Ouch," he said as he stood up. He rubbed his elbow.

"Hmm, maybe we need to practice some more," Buzz called from up on the desk.

Woody took off his wings. The paper was crumpled and torn. "I think we better come up with a new idea," Woody said.

Later that day, Sarge and the Green Army Men tried to help Woody.

"You know what you need, soldier," Sarge said. "Some basic training. The first thing you need to do is bulk up."

"Umm . . . okay," Woody said. "If you think it will impress Bo."

"Excuse me?" Sarge barked.

"I mean, sir, yes, sir!" Woody shouted, standing at attention.

"Let's get started!" Sarge said. "Climb that rope, soldier! Go, go, go!"

Woody tried to climb a long cord that was hanging from the curtains. But he didn't make it very far. "Sarge," Woody called as he dangled above the floor. "Are you sure this is the way to impress Bo?"

Sarge was sure. He made Woody lift barbells and run through an obstacle course. He had him do push-ups and chin-ups and sit-ups.

Woody was exhausted. But he perked up when he saw the perfect opportunity to show Bo his new strength.

Bo was trying to get a book off a shelf, but it was wedged in so tightly that it wouldn't budge.

Woody hurried over to help her. "Allow me," he said.

He pulled the book with all his might, but nothing happened. He pulled again and again but still the book wouldn't move.

Woody felt terrible. All his training had made him too tired to lift a book.

While the Little Green Aliens helped Bo with her book, Woody walked over to the bed. After his workout and flying lesson, he needed a nap.

Wheezy the penguin danced over to Woody. He was singing a cheerful tune.

Woody couldn't help but smile. Then he had an idea. "Hey, Wheezy," he said. "Do you think you could teach me how to sing like that? I'll bet Bo would really get a kick out of it."

"No problem," Wheezy replied. "Let's hear what you've got."

"La, la, la, la, la," screeched Woody.

Wheezy winced. "Not to worry," he reassured Woody. "I've got an idea."

That night, Woody gave Bo her very own concert.

She sat down with her sheep to watch.

Woody began to "sing" a romantic song—but Bo couldn't help noticing that his voice seemed to be coming from somewhere else.

Bo got up, went over to the curtain, and pulled it aside. There was Wheezy, singing away while Woody pretended it was his voice.

"Very funny, you two," Bo said. Then she walked away.

Woody didn't know what to try next. He thought that maybe he needed a girl's opinion. The next morning, he decided to ask Jessie what she thought.

"What a gal likes is a guy who's got a lot of enthusiasm!" Jessie said. "Maybe you need to pick up the pace instead of moseyin' around all the time. Really show her you're interested, you know what I mean?"

"Maybe," said Woody. But he wasn't so sure.

"Don't be shy now," Jessie coached him. "Go lasso that pretty little gal of yours before someone else does!"

The next time Woody saw Bo, he tried out his new act. "Hi, Bo!" he shouted. "It's a beautiful day, isn't it? That's a lovely dress you're wearing. How are those sheep of yours? You sure do take good care of them!" Then he linked his arm through Bo's and swung her around. "Yee-ha!" Woody exclaimed. "Has anyone ever told you that you are a spectacular dancer?"

Bo held on to her bonnet as she spun around. When Woody finally let her go, she looked at him, concerned. "Woody, I think your string may be wound too tight. Do you want me to take a look at it?"

Woody's face turned red. He didn't want Bo to think there was something wrong with him! He tried to smile and then hurried away.

Later that day, Hamm gave Woody some advice. "Listen," Hamm said. "A lot of ladies like the strong silent type. The less you say, the more she'll want to talk to you."

"Are you sure?" asked Woody.

"Absolutely," said Hamm. "Look, here she comes now!"

Woody nodded. He was ready to try anything.

"Hi, Woody," said Bo. "Have you seen my sheep?"

Woody just tipped his hat and smiled.

"Is that a yes or a no?" Bo asked.

When Woody didn't reply again, she shouted, "Woody! Can you hear me?"

Woody didn't say a word. He adjusted the bandana around his neck.

Bo looked at him, puzzled. Then she walked away.

Woody was starting to wonder if his friends' advice was really any good.

Rex could see his friend was still upset. "I hope I'm not being too personal here," he said, "but why don't you just ask Bo what she's looking for in a man. Then you'll know what impresses her."

"Rex!" exclaimed Woody. "That's a brilliant idea!"

"Thank you," replied Rex. "It's nice to be known for my brains as well as for my brute strength."

Woody went straight over to Bo and asked her.

"Well," Bo answered, "I like a guy who is kind and smart and funny. Someone who is a good friend. And someone who isn't afraid to be himself."

"Um . . . have you ever met anyone like that?" Woody asked.

"Oh, Woody!" Bo cried. "Of course I have! It's you! Although you really haven't been yourself lately."

"I guess I was trying to get you to like me even more," Woody admitted.

"Impossible," said Bo. She planted a kiss on his cheek.

That night, Woody brought Bo a beautiful bouquet of flowers. "Would you care to join me for a stroll?" he asked.

"I'd be delighted," answered Bo.

Soon the pair were talking and laughing and having a wonderful time.

"Now this is the Woody I've been missing," said Bo.

"Well, get used to him," said Woody. "'Cause he's here to stay."

Bo gave Woody's arm a squeeze. "I'm glad," she said, "because so am I."

Toys in Paradise

Andy ran around his room, throwing clothes into a bag. He would be leaving any minute. His best friend's family was going to Florida on vacation and had invited him to come along.

"You're going to have so much fun!" Andy's mother exclaimed as she helped him pack. "You'll go to the beach and to amusement parks. I wish Molly and I could come along!"

After Andy and his mother left the room, Andy's toys came to life. They gathered on the floor beside Andy's bed where a travel pamphlet lay.

"I'd give anything to go on a tropical vacation," said Bo Peep. "Just think of it. The sandy beaches, the blue ocean, the warm sunshine."

"Not me," Rex the dinosaur said. "There are *sharks* in the ocean. And what about *sunburn*?"

"Hey, I've got an idea," said Jessie the cowgirl. "Why don't we make our own tropical paradise, right here in Andy's room?"

"We wouldn't even have to fly," said Rex. He sighed in relief.

"I could use some downtime," Slinky Dog admitted. "I've been feeling stretched to my limit lately."

"Yippee!" Jessie cried. "What do you think we'll need?"

"This might help," Woody suggested. The toys gathered around as he flipped open the pamphlet. "Andy's mom left it behind. This is where Andy is staying."

"Lounge chairs, umbrellas, water," Buzz Lightyear the space ranger said. "We can find all this stuff right here."

Sarge and the Green Army Men went in search of a potted plant. Hamm and Rex raided the kitchen for Buster's water dish and some sponges. Bo found a doll parasol in Molly's room.

Soon, all the supplies were gathered in the center of the room.

"Next stop: paradise!" Jessie exclaimed.

In no time at all, the toys *had* created their own tropical paradise.

"Ahh, this is the life," Woody said with a sigh. He and Buzz were stretched out on the lounge chairs they had made out of shoebox tops and sponges.

"Wait a minute," Jessie said. "We forgot the sun."

"We can't forget the sun!" exclaimed Buzz. "Our planet—"

"The *pretend* sun," Woody reminded him.

"Oh, right," Buzz replied. "I know just what we need." He dragged Andy's desk lamp to the edge of the desk and turned it on. "Better put on some shades."

Rex and Hamm were by the makeshift ocean. Hamm looked a little sad. "What's an ocean without any waves?" he said.

Woody and Buzz hopped off their lounge chairs. They each grabbed a side of the ocean and started tilting it up and down.

"Surf's up!" announced Woody.

Jessie enjoyed a lively game of volleyball with Bullseye. Afterward, she sat by the water and admired the view. Then she realized something was missing—an ocean breeze!

She got up and lassoed a knob on Andy's dresser. Once the rope was secure, she began to climb. When she made it to the top, she flipped a switch.

A slight breeze started.

"What's that?" Woody said.

Within seconds, the wind picked up, blowing things everywhere. The toys scurried for cover as the parasol and the beach chairs skittered across the room.

"Typhoon!" Rex cried, diving under the bed.

"It's okay!" Jessie called. She flipped off the switch, and the wind stopped. "It was just the fan. Is everyone okay?"

"Almost everyone," Woody said. He pointed toward the bed where Rex's tail poked out from under the bedspread.

It took a little while, but finally, Jessie and the rest of the toys convinced Rex to come out of his hiding place. He was still trembling with fear.

"I don't think I can survive another relaxing vacation!" the dinosaur said.

"Don't worry, Rex," Woody said. "There won't be any more storms here today."

"Woody's right," Jessie chimed in. She put the parasol back in its place, shading the lounge chairs from the "sun". "We're in for clear skies and warm weather."

Rex walked back over to the beach. "I hope Andy has a great trip," he said. "Because paradise can be fun . . . as long as you're with good friends."

Showdown!

Jessie the cowgirl was watching TV one afternoon when she found a *Woody's Roundup* special on the Western Channel. She settled in to watch the episode. . . .

In the old Wild West, Jessie was walking across the Okeydokey Corral when the wind lifted her hat right off her head. She raced after it, but her hat landed high atop a prickly cactus!

"Rotten rattlesnakes!" Jessie cried. She tried roping the hat with her lasso. But it kept looping around one of the cactus's arms.

"Doggone it!" Jessie exclaimed.

Sheriff Woody came over. "What's going on?" he asked.

Jessie pointed to her hat and told Woody what had happened.

"I'll get it for you," Woody said. He threw some peanuts up at the cactus. They landed on the hat's wide brim.

Jessie watched as a couple of black crows swooped toward the cactus. "How is that supposed to help?" she asked.

As the crows grabbed at the peanuts, they knocked the hat off the cactus. It tumbled into Jessie's arms.

"Good thinking, Woody," Jessie said as she put her hat on. "Thanks for the hand!"

"That's why I'm sheriff," Woody said. "It's my job to take care of folks."

"I can take care of myself," Jessie replied.

"No offense, Jessie," Woody said. "I just meant that I step in when ordinary cowpokes need help."

"Hey, I'm no ordinary cowpoke, buster!" Jessie shouted.

Woody shrugged. "There's nothing wrong with being ordinary."

"I can out-cowpoke you any day," Jessie said. "Let's just see who is the better cowpoke."

Woody smiled. “Who cares,” he said. “We’re both good cowpokes. Let’s forget it.”

“Why, are you chicken?” Jessie asked with a smile.

“No, ma’am!” Woody replied.

“Bok-bok-bok!” Jessie flapped her arms.

“Quit it, Jessie,” Woody said. “And quit saying you’re the better cowpoke. You couldn’t rope your own hat off a cactus plant.”

“I’ll never stop saying it, because I’m twice the cowpoke you are,” Jessie challenged.

Woody knew Jessie was a great cowpoke. But he didn’t think she was better than him. “No way,” he said. “Everyone knows I’m three times the cowpoke you are.”

"What's all the fussing and feuding about?" the Prospector said as he walked over. Woody's horse, Bullseye, was with him.

"We're just having a chat," Woody replied.

"Right," Jessie said. "A chat about how Sheriff Woody's an overcooked chicken."

Woody sighed. He knew Jessie didn't really think he was chicken. They needed to stop this fighting right now. "Well, Jessie, should I just say you're as good a cowpoke as I am?"

Jessie grinned. That was all she wanted to hear. She knew that Woody was a fine cowpoke. "That's . . ."

"Whoa, hold on a rootin' tootin' minute," the Prospector said. "Doesn't seem like Jessie was asking for an apology, Sheriff. Sounds like she was looking for a challenge. A true cowpoke never backs down from a challenge."

"Well, if Woody admits we're even, I'll let it go," Jessie said.

The Prospector said, "We'll settle this with a contest. Jessie, how will you prove you're the toughest cowpoke in the West?"

Jessie glanced at Bullseye. "A good cowpoke knows how to talk to a horse," she said. "Let's see who teaches Bullseye the best trick."

"All right," Woody said. "Ladies first."

Jessie walked up to the horse. "Sit, Bullseye." Bullseye just snorted at her.

"Time's up," the Prospector declared. "Sheriff, your turn!"

"Okay, Bullseye, shake," Woody said. Bullseye sniffed Woody's hand.

"Sorry," Jessie said. "Looks like your horse is a no-trick pony."

"I think you're right," Woody said. "What do you say we call it a draw?"

"I've got it," the Prospector exclaimed. "We'll see who can ride Ol' Diablo."

Ol' Diablo was a fat, lazy bull. Jessie stared at him sleeping in the cool grass.

"You're first this time," Jessie said.

Woody hopped onto the bull's back. "Giddy-up!"

Ol' Diablo sank to the ground and closed his eyes.

"Get up, you lazy bull!" he yelled.

Jessie laughed. "Pretty fancy bulldozing, Sheriff."

Woody scowled. "Can you do better?"

"No problem," Jessie said. She climbed up on the bull's back.

Ol' Diablo sat straight up, sending Jessie tumbling down a hill.

The Prospector chuckled.

"How else can we prove who's the roughest, toughest cowpoke?" Jessie asked.

"Since you can't get the bull to shake a leg, you'll have to shake, rattle, and roll yourselves in a square-dancing contest," the Prospector said. He ran off to do some work while they practiced.

“Fiddlesticks,” Jessie muttered. She was worried about facing Woody in a dance contest. She watched him warm up. His feet moved so fast, Jessie was dizzy.

They practiced for a long time. They both wanted to win the contest. Jessie started swinging and swaying around, while Woody did a cowboy jig.

“Wow, you’re a good dancer,” Woody said, stopping to stare.

“Thanks,” Jessie said. She stopped dancing. “You, too.”

Woody smiled. “This contest stuff is dumb. What if . . .”

"Woody! Jessie!" the Prospector called as he came running over. "The new calf just fell into the Rushing River."

"Oh, no!" Jessie cried.

Woody whistled for Bullseye, who galloped toward them. The two cowpokes climbed on his back and raced to the river. Bullseye galloped as fast as he could and skidded to a stop on the riverbank.

Woody and Jessie jumped down and looked around. They spotted the calf wedged against a rock and caught in the current. He was struggling and mooing.

"He's stuck and trying to get loose," Jessie said. "He could be swept downstream."

"We have to get him out and keep the current from pulling him away," Woody said.

Jessie grabbed her lasso. She aimed at the calf and let it fly. It landed neatly around the calf's neck.

Woody and Jessie pulled on the rope, but the calf wouldn't budge.

"How will we get him out?" Jessie said.

Woody pointed to some river rocks. "Maybe I can hop across on those and lead him out."

"Be careful," Jessie said. "When you get to the calf, Bullseye and I will help pull."

"Here goes," Woody said, carefully hopping from one slippery rock to the next. Finally, Woody reached the last rock. "Let's go," he said, patting the calf. Woody hopped back across on the rocks, leading the calf all the way.

On the riverbank, Jessie and Bullseye held the rope tightly, stopping the current from sweeping the calf downstream.

The calf burst onto the shore. He ran over to Jessie and licked her cheek. Woody climbed over the last rock and made it onto the shore a minute later.

"Yee-hah!" Jessie exclaimed. "You saved the calf."

"What happened?" asked the Prospector. He was up high on the bank with Ol' Diablo.

"Woody saved the day!" Jessie exclaimed as she hugged the calf. "He's the bravest cowpoke ever."

"Jessie's the real hero," said Woody. "She lassoed the calf like a great cowpoke."

"Seems we still don't know who is the roughest, toughest cowpoke in the West," said the Prospector.

"Yes, we do," said Woody and Jessie together.

"Well, who is it?" the Prospector cried.

Jessie and Woody grinned.

"We're both great cowpokes," Jessie said. "Right, pardner?"

"Right," Woody agreed. "We really are the roughest, toughest team the West has ever seen!"

A Roaring Field Trip

Andy's mom opened the door to his room and stuck her head inside. "Knock-knock!" she said. "Laundry delivery!"

"Did you wash my solar system T-shirt?" asked Andy. "I want to wear it to the science museum tomorrow."

"Sure did," his mom answered. "You're pretty excited about this field trip, aren't you?"

"Oh, yeah!" Andy replied. "They've got a brand-new dinosaur exhibit. And our teacher says if there's enough time, we can even go to the gift shop."

"Well, let's go find my purse and I'll give you some spending money to take along," said his mother.

"Gee, thanks, Mom!" Andy replied as he followed her downstairs.

"Oh, no!" Rex the dinosaur wailed. "She's giving him money! To spend in the gift shop! You know what's in a gift shop, don't you? Toys! What if he picks one he likes better than us? What if he picks a dinosaur fiercer than me? What are we going to do?"

"Calm down," Woody the cowboy told him. "You're right, though, I don't like the idea of the gift shop either."

"Sounds like Andy needs a couple of shopping buddies," added Buzz Lightyear the space ranger.

"Are you suggesting we go to the museum?" Woody asked.

"Why not?" said Buzz. "We might even learn something while we're there."

The next morning, while Andy was having breakfast, Woody and Buzz climbed inside his backpack for their big trip.

"Wait, wait!" yelled Rex. "I'm coming, too! Didn't you hear Andy mention that dinosaur exhibit? This is a once-in-a-lifetime opportunity!" Before Woody or Buzz could say anything, Rex had crammed himself in beside them.

"Good luck!" cried Hamm the piggy bank. "And stay safe!"

"It's a museum," Woody replied. "How dangerous could it be?"

When Andy's class arrived at the museum, he and his classmates excitedly followed their teacher inside.

"Welcome," said their guide. "We're so happy to have you with us today. Before we begin our tour, I'll need you to put your backpacks in the coatroom. You may pick them up at the end of your visit."

The toys looked at each other in alarm. They felt the bag drop to the floor. When the shuffle of feet had grown distant, Woody opened the backpack. Sure enough, they were in the coatroom. And Andy was nowhere in sight.

"Well, that's that," said Woody. "I guess we're stuck here until Andy gets back."

"I didn't come all this way to sit in a coatroom," Buzz said.

"Yeah, this is my one chance to learn how to be a fiercer dinosaur!" Rex cried.

"We just can't go running all over the museum," Woody said.

Rex and Buzz unzipped the backpack and jumped out.

Woody sighed. "If you insist on doing this, then at least let's think it through first," he said.

"Good thinking, Woody," Buzz replied. "First we've got to figure out where we're going."

"To the dinosaurs!" said Rex. He had found a stack of maps behind the counter and was busy studying one. "See? There's a little dinosaur symbol marking where the exhibit is."

"Good work," said Buzz. "Now all we have to do is cover ourselves up with the map and make our way across the lobby."

Ever so carefully, the toys moved slowly across the first floor of the museum.

The Science Museum
Map

"There it is!" Rex said suddenly.

In front of them, behind a huge panel of glass, dinosaurs roared, flicked their tails, and munched leaves. They looked real.

"Oh, my goodness, it's even more magnificent than I expected!" Rex exclaimed. "I've got to get a closer look!"

"No, wait!" called Woody. But Rex was already gone. Seconds later, Woody and Buzz watched in horror as Rex appeared behind the glass.

"Look, a tour group!" whispered Woody. "Hide!"

Woody and Buzz snuck into the exhibit and dove behind some plants. But Rex didn't have time to hide. Instead, he began to move stiffly in place, mimicking the other dinosaurs.

"What kind of dinosaur is that?" asked a boy, pointing at Rex. "I've never seen one so small!"

"I don't know," the tour guide answered. "It must be one of those newly discovered species."

When the coast was clear, Woody and Buzz hustled Rex out of the exhibit and back under the map.

"That was incredible!" Rex declared. "I think I finally found my inner beast!"

"I'm very happy for you," said Woody. "Now let's get back to the coatroom!"

Just then, Buzz spotted a sign: OUTER SPACE EXHIBIT! "Let's go!" he said.

Before Woody could stop him, Buzz was jumping into the basket of a passing stroller.

Woody and Rex dove into the tote bag of a woman heading for the escalator and soon caught up with Buzz outside the planetarium.

"Buzz, we don't have time for this!" scolded Woody.

"Sure we do," said Buzz. "Look, they're closing the doors!" The three friends raced inside just in time.

"Phew!" said Buzz when they were safely inside.

The toys walked through the dark empty theater and climbed into a seat. Suddenly, the ceiling lit up. Planets, moons, and stars moved in the sky above them.

"Wow," Rex whispered. "It's beautiful!"

"That, my friend, is our solar system," said Buzz. "The planet closest to the sun is Mercury. Then come Venus, Earth, Mars, Jupiter, Saturn, Uranus, and Neptune."

"Why is Mars red?" Rex asked.

"Because its soil has a lot of iron," answered Buzz. "When the iron rusts, the dirt turns red."

"And what's that around Saturn?" wondered the dinosaur.

"Those are rings made of billions of particles of ice and rock," Buzz explained.

"All this is extremely informative," said Woody. "But isn't anyone the slightest bit worried that Andy might get back to the coatroom before we do?"

"Negative," replied Buzz. "Did you take a good look at that map? We've got hours before Andy's class is done seeing everything."

The space show was longer than the toys expected. When it was over, a voice came on the loudspeaker: "Your attention, please. The museum will be closing in five minutes."

"We'll never make it back there in time!" cried Woody. The toys raced out of the planetarium. "Andy's going to leave without us!"

"No, he's not," replied Buzz. "Not when we've got a spaceship." He pointed to a model suspended from the ceiling. "Follow me!"

The rest of the museum visitors had emptied out of the second floor by the time Buzz led his friends in a mad dash for the escalator. "Just do what I do!" directed Buzz. He grabbed the handrail, rode it to just above the spaceship, jumped, and dropped inside. Woody followed—but Rex froze.

"You can do it!" Woody yelled from below. "You're the king of the dinosaurs!"

"I think I'm about to become extinct!" Rex wailed as he fell toward the spaceship.

"All right," said Buzz. "Now all we have to do is watch the front door for Andy's class."

"Here they come!" shouted Woody.

"Everybody, lean forward!" Buzz commanded.

Slowly, the spaceship started to move. "Harder! Lean harder!" he yelled.

The spaceship picked up speed, zipping along the cable that attached it to the ceiling.

"Okay," said Buzz, "we've got to wait until we are almost directly above Andy's backpack before exiting the ship."

"*Exiting*?" asked Rex. "Don't you mean falling to our deaths?"

"Now!" shouted Woody. The spaceship was directly above Andy's open backpack. "Abandon ship!"

The toys jumped. Seconds later, they landed softly on the sweatshirt Andy had shoved inside his backpack that morning.

"Thank goodness that child is never cold," Buzz said.

Andy

“Look,” said Woody when they were safely tucked in the backpack. “A bag from the gift shop!”

“What’s in it?” Rex asked nervously.

The toys all looked at the bag, wondering what was inside.

“There’s only one way to find out,” Woody finally said. Slowly, he opened the bag.

“Well?” Buzz asked.

Woody broke into a grin. “What do you know? It’s a big roll of stickers!” he exclaimed.

“Now that’s what I call a good choice!” Rex said.

“Good?” Buzz replied with a smile. “It’s out of this world!”

The Best Hat in the West

It was Saturday morning, and the toys in Andy's room were just waking up. Jessie the cowgirl yawned and stretched her arms. She glanced at the clock. "We almost slept in!" she told Bullseye. "It's time for our favorite show!"

She and the horse hurried over to the TV and switched it on. "It's time for *Woody's Roundup*." Jessie sang along with the show's theme song.

When the episode began, Sheriff Woody and his horse, Bullseye, were chasing down a stray cow.

"Go, Bullseye, go!" Woody called out. Just then, Woody's hat flew off and Bullseye trampled it. "Slow down there, pardner!"

Bullseye stopped, and Woody climbed down to pick up his hat. "Oh, no," he said.

Then Jessie walked up. "Your hat is looking pretty ragged, there, Sheriff," she said.

"I guess so," Woody replied. "I think it's time for a new one."

"I have lots of hats," Jessie offered. "You can take your pick." She brought Woody all the hats she could carry. They were all shapes and colors. They tumbled out of her arms and on to the ground.

Woody looked at all the hats. "How do I pick?" he asked.

"Well," Jessie replied, "just try some of them on. I reckon one will tickle your fancy."

Woody picked up one of the hats and put it on his head. "What do you think?" he asked Jessie and Bullseye.

Bullseye smiled and nodded.

"I think he likes it," Jessie said. "Me, too. It looks mighty fine."

"I don't know," Woody said, looking around at the other hats. "Do you think it's too brown?"

"How about that one?" Jessie said, gesturing toward a hat with buttons on the band. "It's a lighter brown."

"That one is not brown enough," Woody said.

"Hmm," Jessie sighed.

"All right, Woody," Jessie said. She piled more and more hats onto Woody's lap. "There must be a hat here that you like. Keep trying."

Jessie and Woody were making a mess. Bullseye couldn't watch. He covered his eyes.

"I don't think I could wear a hat with a purple band out on the range," Woody said.

"How about this one?" Jessie asked, tossing another hat to Woody.

"That one is pink!" he said.

Jessie put three hats on her own head. "What about a brown one with a gold band? Blue with green? A purple hat with a yellow bow?"

"No, no, no," Woody said. "I'm sorry, Jessie, but none of those are right for me."

Jessie couldn't believe that Woody couldn't find one hat he

liked in the huge pile she had brought. She looked at the hats on the ground.

"Don't give up, Woody," she said. "There are still a lot of hats left."

"What we really need is a plan," Jessie said.

Woody was tired. He'd been trying on hats for over an hour! "Okay, Jessie, I'm willing to try anything. What's your plan?"

"Why don't you tell me just what kind of hat you're looking for," Jessie said. "Then we can try to find it in the pile."

Woody leaned against the fence and thought about Jessie's question. "I definitely like a brown hat," Woody said. "Not too dark or too light, but brown is best."

"All right," Jessie said. She smiled at Bullseye, who was digging his nose into the pile of hats.

"It would be nice if it had a wide brim," Woody continued.

"Anything else?" Jessie asked him.

Woody thought hard. "It should have stitching around the edge. But I don't think we'll find anything like that."

Sheriff Woody looked hopeless. Then Bullseye pulled Woody's old hat from the pile!

Jessie laughed when Bullseye held up the hat.

"Woody, I think Bullseye found just the right hat!" Jessie called out.

Bullseye walked up to Woody and nudged his shoulder. Woody turned and looked. It was just like Woody's old hat.

Woody grinned. "Bullseye, old buddy, you did it!" he exclaimed. Woody put the hat on his head. "This is exactly the kind of hat I wanted."

Woody turned and looked at Jessie. "How does it look?" he asked.

"It's the best hat in the West!" Jessie replied.

The Search for Hamm

Woody the cowboy doll opened one eye, then the other. The sun was up and Andy had already left for school. Since the house was quiet, Woody knew that it was safe for the toys to move around. Woody sat upright and stretched. "Good morning!" he called out.

He dropped off Andy's bed and walked around the room, greeting the other toys who were awake.

"How ya doing, Buzz?" Woody asked the space ranger. "Hiya, Rex. Howdy, Bo Peep. Looking good, Slink."

But his footsteps slowed as he came full circle back to Andy's bed. Something was wrong. Woody looked around the room. "Where's Hamm?" he asked. The piggy bank was nowhere in sight.

The toys all stopped what they were doing. Hamm? No one had seen him since last night!

"I heard his coins rattle as he was settling down to sleep," Rex said.

"Did anyone see—or hear—him after that?" Woody asked.

Each toy thought for a minute. Then slowly, they all shook their heads. No one had seen Hamm.

Buzz jumped to his feet. "We must form a search party!" he said. "Remember that time Slinky fell behind the dresser and we didn't find him for two days?"

"That was scary!" Slinky Dog piped up.

"Something like that may have happened to Hamm," Buzz went on. "Let's scope out every inch of this room!"

The toys gathered around Buzz and Woody, who gave each of them a place to search. Jessie and Bullseye checked the toy chest. The Green Army Men climbed the dresser. RC and Rex rolled back the rug. The Little Green Aliens searched around Andy's desk. They even climbed into each drawer to make sure Hamm hadn't been closed inside. Woody and Bo Peep looked under the bed. Bo's sheep went over to the dark corner where the bedspread bunched up.

The aliens found the first sign of Hamm on Andy's desk. "Oooh!" they chimed, pointing to a small pile of coins next to the pencil holder.

"Good work!" Woody said. He ran up to the pile. Had Hamm lost his coins? They could have just fallen out. Or they could have been loose change that Andy hadn't put in his piggy bank yet. Or maybe, Andy had decided he didn't need a piggy bank anymore.

Woody exchanged a worried glance with Buzz.

The toys gathered around Woody and Buzz, waiting to hear what they should do next.

"What does this mean?" Slinky Dog asked.

"How could Hamm have lost his coins?" Jessie asked, shaking her head.

"What if Andy doesn't want a piggy bank anymore?" Rex asked nervously.

"Now, hold on a minute," Woody said. He didn't want the other toys to panic. "These couple of coins don't mean anything . . . yet. We need to keep looking."

"Our mission is to explore the whole house to see if our friend has left us anymore clues," Buzz said. "Hamm could be in the kitchen or the attic or the laundry room. . . . But if he's anywhere in this house we'll find him!"

"Everyone needs a buddy," Woody said as the toys moved toward the door of Andy's room. "We don't want any more lost toys out there. And when you've finished searching your area, meet us right back here."

Before the toys went off to search, Bo Peep came over to Woody. "Good luck, Sheriff," she said. She gave him a kiss on the cheek. "I know you'll bring Hamm home safely."

Sarge and the Green Army Men were first down the stairs. They moved slowly, hardly making a sound. But the other toys clattered behind them, with Buzz charging down the stairs after Slinky Dog, whose coils clinked with each step. The Little Green Aliens took the steps one at a time.

At the bottom of the stairs, the toys spread out around the house. Rex searched the pantry. Wheezy and the aliens went to the kitchen. Woody and Buzz went to the living room with Sarge and his men.

Before Woody and Buzz could begin to search the living room for clues, they heard a cry.

"Waaaah," Rex wailed from the hallway. "This isn't good."

Woody and Buzz raced out to the hallway. They saw the dinosaur standing beside a pile of coins—three pennies and a quarter. At first, Woody couldn't see anything different about this pile. Then he bent down to pick up a coin. They were wet.

"What is it?" Buzz asked as Woody turned the coin over in his hands. "Do you think it's dog slobber?"

"What?" Rex cried. "You mean Buster took Hamm? Oh, no! I always knew that dog was out to get one of us. And now he has! Oh, poor Hamm!"

"Calm down, Rex," Woody said, trying to stay calm himself. He didn't want to alarm the other toys until they had more information. "Before we tell the others about this pile, let's see what other clues we can find."

Woody walked into the living room with Buzz and Rex. "Any signs of Hamm?" he called out.

"Sir, yes sir!" Sarge responded. He and his men were on the couch. "The troops have found a trace of the missing-in-action toy up here," Sarge said.

Buzz and Woody climbed up on the couch. On the cushions was a cluster of coins. Woody added them up. "Thirteen cents," he said and shook his head. "Poor Hamm!"

Buzz turned to Sarge. "We also found something in the hallway," he said in a low voice. "There were some coins that were . . . wet."

"Wet?" Sarge yelled.

"Shhh," Buzz hissed. "Just come take a look."

They had just jumped down off the couch when one of the Green Army Men sounded the alarm. "Car!" he shouted. "In the driveway—coming fast! It's Andy and his mom."

Woody looked at Buzz, and Buzz looked at Woody. "Upstairs! Quick!" Woody yelled. All the toys raced up the steps as fast as they could. Just as they slid into their places in Andy's room, they heard the front door slam.

Seconds later, Andy dashed into the room. He threw his backpack on the floor, then ran to his toy box. He tossed aside some blocks and other toys until he found what he was looking for. "Here it is!" he said, pulling out his baseball and glove. He ran back out of the room again.

When the coast was clear, the toys came back to life. They all turned to look at Woody.

"What's the plan now, Sheriff?" Buzz asked.

"We'll have to wait until night to search the rest of the house, including the basement," Woody said. His shoulders drooped. What if they never found Hamm?

The toys fell silent. Then, they heard a noise—*clink, clink, clank, clink.*

"What was that?" Rex asked. Woody turned his head. The noise was coming from Andy's backpack.

Clink, clank, clink. It sounded like . . . coins.

Woody rushed over and unzipped the backpack. Out tumbled Hamm!

"Hamm, you big pink pig!" Woody said. "What were you doing in there?"

"Andy took me to school to collect money for a soccer fundraiser," Hamm said. He gave a proud rattle. "Just listen to all that change. This is one happy pig!"

"But we thought you were in trouble," Buzz said. "There were piles of coins all over the house."

"Oh, that was just Andy playing," Hamm replied. "He was tossing me in the air like a baseball when we left this morning. And Buster was following us, drooling everywhere. That dog needs some toys."

"Well, it's sure good to have you back," Woody said. "Andy's room just wasn't the same without you."

So Long, Partner

Over the years, Andy had had a lot of fun playing with his toys. He set up an old Western town in his bedroom and played battle the bandits with them. Sheriff Woody, the cowboy doll, always saved the day.

Andy used his Buzz Lightyear action figure to teach the other toys to "fly". He would swoop the space ranger around the backyard with Jessie the cowgirl and Bullseye the horse. Then he'd have the toys save the galaxy from Buzz's enemy, the evil Emperor Zurg!

At birthday parties or scary-movie nights, Andy would bring along his toys to join in the fun. Woody or Buzz went with him everywhere: to the park, to Pizza Planet, or to a friend's house for a sleepover. And after a long day of fun and adventure, Andy would fall asleep next to his old pals and dream about all the games they would play the next day.

The years passed quickly and before the toys knew it, Andy was getting ready to go to college.

The toys had known this day was coming. But knowing didn't make them any less scared.

"No one's getting thrown out," Woody assured his friends. "We're all still here! Through every yard sale, every spring cleaning, Andy held on to us."

When Andy's mom came upstairs to help Andy pack, she said that anything not packed for college or put in a bag for the attic would be thrown out.

"No one's going to want those old toys," Andy said. He put Jessie, Rex, the Little Green Aliens, and some other toys in a garbage bag to go up to the attic.

Then he picked up Woody and Buzz. He looked first at Buzz. Then at Woody. With a sigh, he put Woody in a box marked COLLEGE. Then he tossed Buzz into the bag.

But Andy's mom threw out the trash bag with the toys inside by mistake.

Luckily, the toys escaped from the bag and ran into the garage. They climbed into a box in the back of the car. It was filled with some old toys that would be taken to a day-care center.

Buzz hesitated. "What about Woody?"

"Andy's takin' him to college!" Jessie said. "We need to go!"

Woody had followed his friends outside to rescue them. He tried to convince them that Andy wanted to put them in the attic. But the other toys wouldn't listen. They wanted to go to the day-care center to be played with. Woody went with them, hoping he could change their minds.

When the toys arrived at Sunnyside Daycare they saw kids playing everywhere. "We hit the jackpot, Bullseye!" Jessie said.

"Well, hello there! Welcome to Sunnyside, folks!" said a pink plush teddy bear. "Please, call me Lotso."

Lotso explained that at Sunnyside, toys were played with every day. There were always new kids to love them.

But Woody didn't want to make a new kid happy. "You have a kid—Andy," he reminded the others. "If he wants us at college, or in the attic, well, then that's where we should be. Now, I'm going home. C'mon Buzz!"

Buzz didn't move. "Our mission with Andy is complete, Woody."

Jessie crossed her arms. "Wake up! It's over. Andy is all grown up."

The toys glanced sadly at one another.

"I gotta go," Woody told his friends. Then he walked out.

The toys couldn't wait to be played with, but the children were much rougher than they were used to. Slinky was stretched to his limit. Rex's tail was snapped off. Jessie's hair was used as a paintbrush. Hamm was coated with glue and covered with macaroni and glitter. A little boy stuck Buzz's head in his mouth! It was awful.

Thunk! Buzz was tossed onto a windowsill. He peered through the window into another classroom. There, he saw Lotso and some of his friends, like Big Baby and Stretch the rubber octopus, being held gently by some older kids. The children quietly cuddled the toys as they listened to a story. Then someone picked up Buzz and threw him back into the chaos.

That night Buzz went to speak with Lotso about getting moved to the room with the big kids. When he found Lotso and his friends, Buzz overheard the toys talking about him and the rest of Andy's toys.

"All them toys are disposable," said Twitch.

"Chuck 'em," Stretch added.

Buzz had to warn his friends! But Big Baby saw him.

"Stop! Let me go!" Buzz cried as Lotso's gang grabbed him. Seconds later he was tied to a chair. Lotso's gang pushed a button to reset Buzz's memory so he couldn't warn his friends.

Meanwhile, the rest of Andy's toys were recovering from a hard day. They started to think they'd made a terrible mistake by coming to the day-care center. Andy had always loved them, and taken good care of them. They realized that Woody had been right. They were Andy's toys! They didn't belong at Sunnyside.

Jessie hopped up. "Guys—we gotta go home!"

But before they could move, Lotso and his gang came in with Buzz. They herded Andy's toys into storage baskets. Lotso didn't want Andy's toys to leave. In the day-care center, the new toys were for the little kids to play roughly with. Lotso and his friends didn't want to get dipped in paint and pulled apart!

Jessie looked at Buzz. He would save them!

Except Buzz didn't even seem to know his old friends. He tackled Rex and then knocked down the other toys. "Prisoners, disabled, Commander Lotso!" he said.

Andy's toys looked at each other. What had happened to Buzz?

After Woody had left Sunnyside, he'd been taken home by a little girl named Bonnie. Her toys knew all about Lotso. They told Woody that Lotso had once belonged to a girl named Daisy. Daisy accidentally left Lotso at a rest stop. Lotso never forgave her for leaving him behind.

Woody hid in Bonnie's backpack so he could get back to the day-care center. He had to save his friends!

When Woody got to Sunnyside, his friends told him everything that had happened.

"From now on, we stick together. We're busting out of here tonight," Woody said. Then he told them his plan.

First, they found Buzz. Woody pushed another button and Buzz started speaking Spanish. But he was on their side again! Then, they snuck outside.

Big Baby was on the swing. The toys crept across the playground behind him, heading for the trash chute.

But Lotso was waiting for them. "What are you all doing? Running back to your kid?" Lotso asked. "He doesn't want you!"

Soon Lotso ended up in the Dumpster. He tried to pull Woody in after him. When Andy's toys went to help Woody, they all tumbled in.

Before they could climb out of the Dumpster, the garbage truck came to pick up the trash. After a bumpy ride, Buzz snapped back to his old self. But the toys were dumped onto a moving conveyor belt headed for the shredder!

Jessie spotted a magnetic belt. The toys began grabbing metal objects that lifted them onto the magnetic belt. But then they were trapped on a new belt, headed toward a fire. Lotso appeared in front of the emergency stop button.

"Push it!" Woody yelled. But Lotso just laughed and ran away.

"Buzz, what do we do?" Jessie asked. Buzz took her hand. The toys closed their eyes as they got closer to the fire.

A shadow passed over Woody's face. He opened his eyes. A giant claw was lowering itself over the toys' heads. The jaws opened and picked everyone up.

"The Claw!" squeaked the Aliens as they manned the controls. They had seen the claw as soon as they landed in the trash. They always knew it would help them get home!

At last, the toys made it back to Andy's. Everyone climbed into the ATTIC box as Woody and Buzz said good-bye.

Then Woody had an idea. He stuck a note on the box with Bonnie's address.

Andy took the box to Bonnie's house. "These are my toys," he told Bonnie. "I need someone really special to play with them."

He showed Bonnie each toy. Then he came to Woody. "What's he doing in here? He's been my pal for as long as I can remember." Andy smiled. Giving Woody one last squeeze, Andy handed Woody to Bonnie. Then he got in his car.

Bonnie went inside with her mother. The toys sat together, watching Andy drive away. "So long, partner," Woody said.

Buzz put his arm around Woody's shoulders. Even though they didn't have Andy, they knew everything would be just fine. After all, they had each other. And a new kid who'd love them the way Andy had.

THE END